CW01459285

MILLION TO ONE CHANCE

By

Trevor Hodson

Order this book online at www.trafford.com/06-1375
or email orders@trafford.com

Most Trafford titles are also available at major online book retailers.

© Copyright 2007 Trevor J. Hodson
All rights reserved. No part of this publication may be reproduced, stored in a retrieval system, or
transmitted, in any form or by any means, electronic, mechanical, photocopying, recording, or
otherwise, without the written prior permission of the author.

Note for Librarians: A cataloguing record for this book is available from Library
and Archives Canada at www.collectionscanada.ca/amicus/index-e.html

Printed in Victoria, BC, Canada.

ISBN: 978-1-4120-9619-5

*We at Trafford believe that it is the responsibility of us all, as both individuals
and corporations, to make choices that are environmentally and socially sound.
You, in turn, are supporting this responsible conduct each time you purchase a
Trafford book, or make use of our publishing services. To find out how you are
helping, please visit www.trafford.com/responsiblepublishing.html*

*Our mission is to efficiently provide the world's finest, most comprehensive
book publishing service, enabling every author to experience success.
To find out how to publish your book, your way, and have it available
worldwide, visit us online at www.trafford.com/10510*

Trafford
PUBLISHING™

www.trafford.com

North America & international
toll-free: 1 888 232 4444 (USA & Canada)
phone: 250 383 6864 ♦ fax: 250 383 6804
email: info@trafford.com

The United Kingdom & Europe
phone: +44 (0)1865 722 113 ♦ local rate: 0845 230 9601
facsimile: +44 (0)1865 722 868 ♦ email: info.uk@trafford.com

10 9 8 7 6 5 4 3

Foreword

Are you looking forward to your Holiday? All the Sun, Sea, and Sand, but not looking forward to the flight?

Do you hate flying, but put up with it to enable you to get where you want to go?
How would you react then, if you had no choice, but to fly an Airliner with the lives of 150 people including your own family in your hands?

Although some of the events in this Novel are based on true events, the names of the characters are the figment of the author's imagination, as he relives the lives of ordinary people, doing ordinary things, and not expecting to have to do extra ordinary activities with very serious outcomes if things go wrong, or is it a 'Million to one Chance' of ever happening.

You will have to judge for yourself.

The Osborn family are just an ordinary family doing ordinary things like you.

But imagine the impossible happening, could you cope.

Chapter 1

Ringgggggggggggggggggggggg,   Ringggggggggggggggggggggggg,
Ringggggggggggggggggggg, Ringgggggggggggggggggggggggg, an arm reaches out
and hits the off button on the alarm clock. Stuart rolls over towards the centre of
the bed still half-asleep. He slides his hands back under the bedclothes and across
Tricia's warm naked bottom, and around her warm abdomen.

'Get off, don't you dare, your flipping hands are cold,' she scornfully remarks.

'Arr go on I only want a cuddle, I'll warm them.'

'No, it's time we were up anyway, I thought you wanted to be up early today?'

'I do, but a little lovin' wouldn't go amiss,' he replied.

'One thing about being a school teacher is you do get long holidays and a
chance to lie in every now and again,' he said, but there was no reply from
Tricia. It seemed obvious a cuddle was out of the question this morning he
thinks to himself, as he sits up and swings his legs out of bed putting his feet
into his slippers, which had been conveniently placed where he left them the
night before. Standing up and looking out of the bedroom window through a
small chink he had made in the curtains, the early morning summer sunshine
was streaming into the room as he made his way across the landing to the
bathroom.

'No rest for the wicked,' he remarked to himself as he closed the bathroom door.
Having relieved himself, he flushes the toilet and washes his hands and face.
Looking into the mirror as he dries himself off, he says 'you handsome brute
you. I don't know what all the fuss is about, yes I am a little podgy here, and a
little grey there, but still not bad for just over forty,' he mutters.

Stuart and Tricia Osborn have been married for seventeen years, and have two
children. Claire is their first-born, and is fourteen years of age, and a typical
teenage girl, very outspoken for her meagre years, but equally very intelligent.
Their youngest is Craig, who is their seven-year-old son, and the torment of his
sister's life.

'Bathrooms free,' Stuart shouts, as he puts his dressing gown on and descends
the stairs to lay breakfast. The best time of the day is coming down first, and
having breakfast in peace he thinks to himself. He opens the kitchen blind, and
the dining room curtains, and finally the lounge curtains. He admires his well-
manicured lawns, which he has painstakingly cut, and appreciates the effort he

put in with his new lawn mower. The flowerbeds are a blaze with colour of petunias, geraniums and pansies, plus the odd shrub here and there.

He turns round to see Max the mad springer spaniel stretching out, having just woken up from his slumbers and wagging his stumpy little tail. 'Morning Max had a good nights sleep, where's Suzy?' he remarks. Max spins round and dashes out of the lounge into the dining room to see Suzy the tortoiseshell cat leap off the dining table and make a dash for the kitchen and the cat flap in the back door. Max loses his grip as his paws hit the slippery kitchen floor. Suzy dives for the cat flap as Max smashes into the back door.

Max starts barking. 'Okay,' Stuart says as he opens the back door, and Max continues his hunt for the cat up the garden, but Suzy's made for the garage roof, and looks down as Max is barking back at her.

That's the cat out, and the dog has had his exercise for the day, Stuart thinks to himself as he walks into the hall, and pulls the morning newspaper from the letterbox. Now I can read the newspaper, and have some tea in peace.

The kitchen door opens, and in walks Craig his seven-year-old son still in his pyjamas, and rubbing the sleep out of his eyes. 'Hello Son, you're up early.' 'Can I watch TV Dad, Tarzan's on?'

'It's a bit early for TV Son, but go on, but keep the sound down we don't want to wake the neighbours.' 'Can I have a cup of tea and some cornflakes?' Craig asks, as he walks through into the lounge.

'Where's your Mother?' Stuart asks Craig, ' She's in the bathroom.'

Craig reaches down and switches the television on, and sprawls out on the settee, and snuggles down to watch his favourite programme. Stuart enters the lounge carrying Craig's tea and cornflakes.

'Here you are Son, don't spill it.' Craig places the mug of tea on the floor and takes the bowl of cornflakes from his dad. Stuart returns to the dining room and carries on reading the morning paper and takes a sip of tea.

He hears scratching at the back door and a bark, Max has decided to return after his morning watering of the plants. Stuart gets up from the dining table and enters the kitchen, and opens the backdoor. 'I suppose you want your breakfast an' all? Well you will have to wait a minute.' Stuart returns to his newspaper and his breakfast.

Max wanders through to the lounge not looking where he's going, and knocks Craig's mug of tea over as he tries to see what Craig is eating. 'You stupid dog look what you've done, you've knocked my tea over, Dad's going to kill you,' Craig shouts at the top of his voice.

Max comes flying back through the lounge into the dining room and makes a beeline for the kitchen, just as the kitchen door opens and in walks Tricia carrying a basket of washing. Both Tricia and Max collide, Tricia falls to the floor and lands on top of Max. The basket of washing fly's across the kitchen floor and hits the cooker, as Max yelps out.

'You bloody stupid dog,' she shouts. 'What's up now?' Stuart remarks as his breakfast is disturbed yet again. He goes to Tricia's aid and helps her up. 'That dog will be the death of me,' she says.

'Never mind, you'll survive.' 'No thanks to you,' Tricia remarks.

Tricia is Stuart's wife, an attractive petite brunette, and benefits Stuart's life with her light-hearted good nature.

The dog sees his opportunity to escape the melee in the kitchen, and makes a break for the stairs and safety. He bounds up the stairs to Claire's room. Claire is Stuart and Tricia's fourteen-year-old teenage daughter, who appears sweet and angelic on the surface, but has a tendency to be strong willed, and aggressive from time to time, when the mood takes her.

Max enters the room and the bedroom door bangs back, hits the chest of drawers behind the door waking Claire from her sleep. Max takes a flying leap onto her bed, as she lies there with the duvet wrapped round her, half-awake and dreaming of Anthony Jackson in the sixth form. Max licks her face 'Get off you're wet, where the devil have you been?' she says. Max just wags his tail and jumps down from the bed.

'Are you getting up today, your breakfast is ready?' Stuart shouts up to Claire from the bottom of the stairs.

He turns to Tricia 'Do you want some tea love?' 'Please,' she replies. As he pours her tea she sits at the dining table rubbing her knees, although there were no bruises it still hurt. 'It's a nice day for washing,' Stuart remarks. 'Yes, I think there should be two loads, just what I want,' she replies in disgust.

'What are your plans for the day?' she asks Stuart. 'Well, I think I will have a shower and take the dog a walk.' 'Max,' Stuart shouts 'Do you want your breakfast boy?' The kitchen door flies open and in struts Max with his tail wagging. Stuart pours a good portion of winolot out of a packet into Max's bowl, and puts it on the floor.

Claire exits the bathroom, 'It's all yours Dad,' she shouts down.
'Thanks.'

'Just one Cornetto, give it to me,' Stuart sings as he runs upstairs, and closes the bathroom door.

'Oh please, give it a rest Dad,' Claire remarks in a pathetic tone, trying to appeal to his better nature, and to save her hearing from the out of tune singing of her father. 'You'll never make the Albert Hall,' she shouts.

The electric shaver is heard to buzz, followed by more rendering of 'Just one Cornetto.' Stuart opens the shower cubicle door and steps inside and turns the shower on, not looking at what he was doing, as the shower hits him full blast with hot water, followed by 'Who the bloody hell left this on full blast?'

Claire continues to get dressed as Tricia shouts up from downstairs.

'Claire, have you got any more dirty washing for me?' 'Yes Mom, I'll bring it down in a minute.'

Tricia starts to gather the dirty crockery from the dining table and loads the dishwasher.

'Mom,' Craig shouts from the lounge, 'There's my cereal bowl and mug in here.'

'Well bring it through then,' she replies in disgust at the lazy little devil, but there is no response, and she walks through to the lounge.

'Cheers Mom,' Craig thanks his mother. 'Whose spilt tea on the carpet?'

Craig replies, 'It wasn't me, it was Max, he knocked it over.' Tricia returns to the kitchen and gets a floor cloth from the cupboard under the sink, and returns to the lounge to wipe up the tea.

'I hope this comes off?' she explains to Craig, as she starts to rub the area with a damp cloth. 'Sorry Mom,' he replies. 'You're lucky, it's come off.' 'I didn't do it.' Craig protests his innocence at the trouble caused.

Claire enters the kitchen with her dirty washing. 'Put it in the basket,' Tricia remarks as she starts to load the washing machine.

'I suppose you would like your breakfast now miss?' she says to Claire in a sarcastic tone. 'Please Mom,' Claire replies. 'Why we can't all have breakfast at the same time beats me,' Tricia protests.

The kitchen door opens and in walks Stuart, dressed in his sweatshirt, shorts and trainers and commences to do stretching exercises and running on the spot. 'My God, what's this then, going to show the neighbourhood up are we?' Tricia jokingly remarks.

'It's a lovely morning for a run, so come on Max, walkies,' as Max springs out of his basket in the corner of the kitchen, eager for his run as well.

Stuart takes the dogs lead and clips it onto his collar as Max pulls them both out of the back door towards the garden gate. 'All right take it easy, we're not there yet.' Stuart cautiously gets Max to calm down.

The sun is shining and neighbours are out, either mowing lawns or gardening, or washing their cars on this lovely Saturday in early August. It's five past ten and the temperature is already well into the mid- twenties centigrade. Stuart and Max turn left out of the road they live in, and enter the road leading to the park. Max stops dead and sniffs the lamppost on the corner, and leaves his mark against it.

Tricia takes a cup of tea through to the lounge and cuddles up next to Craig. Craig rests his head on his mothers' lap.

'I thought you were going out to play this morning?' Tricia asks Craig.

'I am,' he replies. Tricia strokes Craig's fair hair. 'How's my baby this morning?' she asks.

'Oh Mom, I am not a baby any more, I am seven,' he protests.

'You will always be my baby Son,' she remarks, and has another sip of tea.

'Wasn't you supposed to be playing with Simon?' she asks. 'Yes.'
'Well you can't sit here all day watching TV, so why don't you go and get dressed, and go an' see Simon,' she remarks. 'OK.' He reluctantly gets up from the settee, and goes to his room to get dressed. Tricia turns the TV off and re-enters the kitchen, and puts her mug in the dishwasher and switches it on.

As the dishwasher begins it's washing programme she gazes out of the kitchen window, and stares vacantly into space, allowing her mind to wonder towards sun drenched beaches, when her thoughts were suddenly interrupted as she hears Craig enter the kitchen behind her.

'Did you clean your teeth and behind your ears this morning?' Tricia asks Craig.

'Of course I did,' he says, as he leaves the house via the back door, and walks up to the garage to get his bike to make his way to Simon's house.

'Don't go far, and be back for lunch,' Tricia shouts out to him, as he opens the back gate. 'I won't,' he replies, ' and mind the traffic.'

'He never takes any notice Mom, I don't know why you bother,' Claire says as she walks into the kitchen.

'I am going to Sarah's in a bit Mom, and then we're going into town, do you want anything?' Claire asks her mother.

'No, you're all right we shopped yesterday, but thanks for asking,' Tricia replies.

Stuart and Max are passing David Charles's house, a friend of the family and David is cleaning his car. 'Morning Dave,' Stuart says.

David turns round and leaves his car cleaning.

'Oh hello Stuart, how are we then Max?' Dave says, as he bends down to give the dog some fuss, and Max wags his tail in a pleasing manner.

'He's OK, but he has caused some chaos this morning, he's knocked a mug of tea over, chased the cat out of the house and fetched Tricia down in the kitchen, but other than that he's OK,' Stuart says.

'How are things with you then Dave?' Dave is a retired bank manager who took early retirement due to his own ill health, caused by stress.

'Could be better I suppose. Kath's not well again, but it's no good grumbling they say, there are others worse off than you.'

'Well we must get on Dave, Max is breaking his neck, oh are we still OK for our golfing session on Wednesday?' 'Yes, that I'll be fine, usual time, see you,' Dave replies as Stuart and Max continue their walk towards the park.

Craig reaches Simons house and knocks on the door. The door opens, and Simons mother is standing there. A rather large lady with a bubbly personality, and a warm smile is shown from her rosy cheeks. 'Hello Craig.' 'Is Simon in Mrs Newman?' Craig replies. ' Yes, he's in the lounge playing on his computer, go on through.'

Craig leans his bike against the house, and thanks Mrs Newman as he walks passed her on his way into the lounge. 'Hi Craig,' says Simon.

'I've had this new game 'The Green Eyed Monster' it's really good, grab this stick, two can play,' Craig pulls up a chair.

'It's about a haunted castle, and you have to get to the central keep to get the gold, but watch out for the 'Green Eyed Monster', as traps are round every corner.'

The two boys start playing as Mrs Newman enters the room.

' Would you like a drink Craig?' she asks, 'Yes please,' he replies,

'Lemonade or Coke?' 'Coke please Mrs Newman,' 'Simon would you like one?'

'Please Mom.' The two boys continue their game.

Chapter 2

As Stuart reaches the park gates, he bends down and releases Maxis lead, and the dog dashes off towards the nearest tree. Stuart commences his run round the park with Max trying to keep up; but the distractions are just too great. With other people, and children playing ball, and other dogs, Max is soon left well behind.

Stuart stops, and turns round, unable to see Max he calls his name out, but still no response. He calls again, and again, and again, and finally Max comes running round the corner towards him.

'Where the hell have you been?' Stuart asks Max, 'Chasing other dogs no doubt,' Stuart says.

'Well come on, and keep up.' Stuart starts to run again as Max looks across the lake at some ducks swimming leisurely by, and unable to contain the temptation, he dives straight in after them. The ducks squawk in alarm, and scatter in all directions. Stuart turns round to see Max attempting to catch the ducks; but he is no match for them, and they are long gone before any harm is done.

'Max get out,' Stuart shouts. Max doggy paddles back to the waters edge, and gets out, and shakes himself dry. 'Come on,' Stuart shouts as he continues his jogging.

Tricia's first load of washing has finished, and she starts to empty the machine, and puts it into the washing basket. God, there must be better things in life than this, she thinks to herself. She takes the washing out, and starts to peg it out on the rotary clothesline in the garden. Wouldn't it be nice to be somewhere in the sun other than here, she thinks? Some nice sandy beach with the water lapping over the edge, having suntan lotion rubbed into my skin by a handsome young Spanish Gigolo, sipping a rum and coke. Well, I suppose I can dream.

'Morning Tricia.' Tricia hears a voice from next door over the fence. 'Oh, hello Sandra.'

'It's a lovely day for the washing.' ' Yes, I suppose it is.' ' You don't sound too cheerful.'

'No, I suppose I don't. I was just thinking I would much rather be on a beach by the sea, having suntan lotion rubbed in by a Spanish Gigolo, and sipping a rum and coke.'

'Tricia, you are wicked,' 'I know.' 'Is there room for two on that beach?'

'Yes of course there is.' They both giggle at the thought of such a thing.

'We had a short holiday last month and it was great, plenty of food, and a lovely hotel and beach.' 'Where was this then?'

'We've never been before, Benidorm in Spain, lovely views over the sea, and the beach stretches for miles.' 'I bet it cost a pretty packet?'

'No not really, we had one of those last minute deals off Teletext.'

'I would have trouble convincing Stuart, he likes things organised.'

'It was easy, we made one phone call, and everything was sorted. It was as easy as that.' 'Really, oh well we will have to see,' Tricia remarked.

Sarah and Claire have met each other at Strawberry's Café in town.

'Do you want a Coffee, or a Coke?' Sarah asks Claire. 'I'll get them,' Claire replies.

'No, it's alright, you get us a seat by the window, and we can do some talent spotting.'

'I'll have a Coffee please.' 'Two Coffee's please,' Sarah asks the waitress.

'Two fifty please,' the waitress says, 'I'll bring them over.' 'Thanks.' Sarah joins Claire at the table.

'Well, spotted anyone yet?' 'Yes, that creep Colin Allen, he goes out with Wendy Hall, I don't know what she sees in him, he's a real jerk.'

'Have you seen how he dresses, he looks like something from the Munster's and that hair, great big Punky spikes, he looks like a real prat.' They both fall about laughing. 'Well, he does,' Claire says, when she gets her breath back.

The waitress brings the two coffee's over, and places them at the table.

'I saw Mary Villiers the other day pushing a pram,' Sarah says, 'I wondered why I hadn't seen her at school', Claire replies. 'It's not hers it's her Mothers. Apparently she has had a rough time, and Mary has been helping out ever since her Dad left them for some other woman.' 'Never.'

Tricia starts to reload the washing machine with her second load of the day. She hears the gate latch click, and the gate opens.

Stuart and Max have returned from their walk. 'Wait there,' Stuart says to Max, as he enters the kitchen.

'Hi Love,' he says to Tricia. 'Had a good walk then?' She asks. 'Not bad, Max dived in after the ducks again.'

'Well don't let him in here until he's dried off.'

Stuart reaches down for the dog's water bowl, he throws the old water down the sink and turns the tap on, and refills the bowl with fresh cold water. He takes the water outside to Max. 'Here you are boy, have some of this.'

Max sprawls out in the shade, and has a good drink as Stuart returns to the kitchen to get the dog's towel. He then walks back outside to give Max a good rub down.

As far as Max is concerned this is brilliant, as he starts to wriggle and roll on his back in the grass, kicking his legs out, and biting Stuart whenever he gets the chance. The two of them compete with each other, in as much as Stuart tries to make the best of rubbing as many places as possible, and Max trying to bite as often as he can, but it's all done with the best of friendly intentions.

Stuart leaves Max in the garden to dry off, and returns to the kitchen and puts the towel away.

'Do you want a Coffee?' Tricia asks Stuart, 'Please,' he replies. Tricia fills the kettle with water, and switches it on. Stuart picks the newspaper up from the dining table, where he had left it before he went for his walk, and walks through to the lounge, and flops down on the settee to carry on reading the paper.

The wireless is playing quietly in the dining room, with music from the fifties & sixties on a local radio station. Tricia puts coffee into two mugs, as the kettle completes its boil and switches itself off, the back door swings open and in struts Max. 'I hope you're dry now Max?' Tricia says to him, as Max looks up at her and wags his tail.

She pours the boiling water into the mugs and adds the milk, and stirs them. She walks through to the lounge, and hands Stuart his coffee, and sits in the armchair to drink hers.

After a few minutes of sitting quietly she says, 'I was talking to Sandra this morning,' as she takes a sip from her mug.

'Oh yes, how is she?' Stuart remarks as he turns over another page of the newspaper. 'She's OK.'

'She said they went to Benidorm in Spain last month, and had a great time. Lovely hotel, lovely beach, good food.'

'Oh yes,' Stuart replies as he continues to read his newspaper, not particularly taking any notice of what Tricia is saying.

'Are you listening to what I am saying?'

'Of course I am,' he replies still reading his paper. 'God, you drive me mad, can't you put that paper down and listen to me just for one minute?'

He folds his newspaper up and puts it down. 'I am all yours dear,' he says. Tricia takes another sip of coffee and crosses her legs, but remains silent for a few minutes.

'What I was saying, Sandra had been on holiday to Benidorm.'

'Yes, I heard you say so,' Stuart replies.

'What I was really saying was, can't we go on holiday?'

Chapter 3

'Have you finished your Coffee?' Sarah asks Claire, 'Yes,' she replies.

'Well come on we'll go to Dotty 'P's and see what new fashions there are to tempt us.'

The two girls leave the coffee shop, and walk further into town, and enter the 'Cornflower Shopping Mall.' The mall is very busy, but it is Saturday. As they approach Dotty 'P's they see Wendy Hall and Colin Allen further up the mall.

'Quick,' Claire says to Sarah, 'I don't think they have seen us,' as they make a dash to enter the shop. 'God, that was close,' Sarah says.

The two girls start to look at the clothes on the racks. Picking items up and examining them, trying them against themselves, and putting them back. Claire picks a black dress up off the rack, and looks at the label and size, it's a size 12-price £25, which had been reduced from £50. 'What do you think?' she says to Sarah.

'It looks nice, it would be OK for the end of term Ball next year.'

'That's what I was thinking. It's a pity Tony Jackson won't be there to appreciate it.'

'What's this then, you got a thing for Tony Jackson?'

'Well, not exactly, but he's not bad.'

'I thought he was with Jane Taylor?'

'I know, but from what I've heard, they had a blazing row the other day, and she gave him the elbow. Someone let it slip to her that I liked him.'

'Well, I wonder who that could have been?' Sarah remarks.

'I wonder,' Claire replies as both girls start giggling. 'You're wicked, do you know that Claire Osborn.'

Both girls start to get bored looking at clothes. 'I've seen enough.' Sarah says, 'Lets go to HMV's and have a listen to some CD's.'

As they reach the shop doorway, they pause for a moment, and check to see if Wendy Hall and Colin Allen are anywhere near. The mall is clear, and they leave, walking further up the mall to HMV's.

As they enter the shop, they see Richard Nolan and Peter Knight, fellow pupils from their school, 'Hi Girls,' Richard says.

'Bog off you pair,' Sarah says, 'Err, who's got one on today then?' Peter Knight replies. As the two lads walk towards the door, Richard Nolan lashes out with his right hand and flicks Claire's long hair.

'I'll call the Manager, and tell them you've been shoplifting again,' Claire says.

'Piss off,' he replies. 'Well go on then,' Sarah remarks, as the two lads leave the shop. 'God, those two make me sick.'

The two girls make their way passed the Country and Western racks, and the Sixties albums, towards the Top Ten singles, and slowly look at different labels. Sarah picks a CD up of Wet - Wet - Wet, 'God I like them, and I think they are really sexy, don't you?'

'Yes, let's go and listen to them,' Claire replies, as the two girls make their way over to a listening booth. They put on the headphones and select hit number 5 on the keypad and the music starts to play, both girls start jigging about to the music and laughing at the same time. A few minutes pass by, and Sarah takes her headphones off, followed by Claire, 'I think I'll have this,' she says to Claire.

Both girls walk over to the pay desk, and Sarah pays for the CD, and they return to the Top Ten racks, as Claire continues to look through the various CD's available. However, unable to make her mind up, they both leave the shop.

'Well, I am waiting for an answer?' Tricia says to Stuart.

'I can't make a decision just like that.' 'Why not?' Tricia replies.

'I don't know if we can afford it?'

'We have a bit saved, and the cards have practically nothing on, so what's stopping us?' she remarks.

Stuart picks his newspaper up again, and starts to read it. Tricia gets up from her chair and joins him on the settee, and cuddles up beside him to really start and put the pressure on, by softening him up with her charms. She links her arm through his, and starts to nibble at his ear.

'Go on,' she says. 'No,' he replies. 'I won't have a headache for a week if you say yes,' she remarks.

'A whole week?' 'A whole week.' She turns and kisses him. 'I didn't say which week,' and they both laugh. 'All right, I'll give it some thought.' 'Today?' Tricia asks. 'Today,' Stuart replies.

She leaps up from the settee in an excited and playful mood and chases Max through to the kitchen. 'Daddy says we are going on holiday,' she says to Max.

'No I didn't,' shouts Stuart, 'I said I would think about it.' Tricia whispers to Max, 'He will, I know my charms will work.'

Zap -Zap -Zap- Zing -Zing –Zing. 'Got'ya, I've won,' Simon shouts, as he declares himself the winner of the game.

'Do you want another game?' he says to Craig.

'No thanks, can we have a game of football in your garden?' he asks.

' Yes, I bags to be Beckham, you can be Owen,' he remarks.

Both boys go into the back garden. They chase each other around with the football, as Simon gives the ball a kick to Craig, who hits the ball against the garage wall to score a goal.

'Did you see the match on Tele last night?' Craig says to Simon.

'Yea, and Beckham scored twice, he was great.'

'Are you in our team again next term?' Craig asks. 'I think so,' Simon replies.

'I hope Vaughan's not in it, he's useless.'

The two boys play around for a while longer. 'Your lunch is ready Simon,' Mrs Newman shouts from the kitchen, 'OK Mom,' he replies.

'What are you doing next week?' Craig asks Simon.

'We're going to Disney World in Paris, and we're going on the Tunnel Train and Dad's driving us there,' Simon says.

'Brill,' Craig replies, as he gets to his bike and turns it round. 'See you,' he says to Simon, as he starts to ride his bike back home, and Simon enters his house for lunch.

Craig cycles slowly back home, pondering on Simon's holiday, and wishing he was going away. I'll ask Dad if we can go to Disney World he thinks to himself, as he enters the back garden via the gate. Max starts barking, and runs out to see whose come. Craig puts his bike back in the garage and enters the house with Max jumping up at him.

'What's for dinner Mom?'

'Baked beans on toast if you want,' she says. ' Yes please,' he replies.

'Had a good time at Simons?' she asks. 'Not bad, he's got this new game and we played with it on his computer, and he won.'

'Was Mrs Newman in?'

'Yes, she gave me some Coke. They are going to Disney World in Paris next week, can we go?'

'You'll have to ask your Dad.' Tricia smiles to herself as she starts to prepare lunch.

Craig makes his way through to the lounge to his father. 'Dad, can we go to Disney World in Paris. Simon and his Mom and Dad are going next week?'

'No, what do you think I am, made of money?' he replies.

'Ah go on,' Craig pleads with his father as he flops down on the settee.

'Ah go on Dad,' Tricia shouts from the kitchen, winding Stuart up to make his monumental decision.

'Your lunch is ready Craig,' Tricia shouts from the kitchen, as she walks through to the dining room, and places Craig's plate at the table. She continues through to the lounge, and passes Craig enroute. 'Do you want a sandwich love?' she asks Stuart.

'Please,' he replies. ' Ham, or Cheese, or Chicken?' she asks.

'Decisions, decisions, decisions, Cheese.' 'Coffee as well your Lordship?' Tricia sarcastically remarks.

He sticks his tongue out at her. 'I'll take it as a yes then.' She leaves the lounge, and returns to the kitchen, and continues to make their lunch.

'Where's Claire?' Craig asks his mother. 'She's gone to town with Sarah.'

Craig carries on eating his lunch. 'If we go on holiday, can I have some new trainers?' Craig asks his mother.

'We'll see, now you know what I've told you about talking and eating at the same time,' she says.

'The frog 'ill get stuck in your throat,' he says. ' Well just be quiet then.'

'Your lunch is ready Stuart,' she says, as she places their lunch at table.

Stuart walks through from the lounge and sits at the table, and they both begin to eat their lunch. Craig finishes his beans on toast, and puts his knife and fork together on his cleaned plate.

He takes a drink of Dandelion and Burdock. He wipes his mouth on the back of his hand and smacks the roof of his mouth with his tongue and sighs.

'Thanks Mom, that was great.' 'May I leave the table please?' he asks his mother.

'Yes, what are you going to do now?' she asks.

'I am just going up the garden to kick the ball around'. He leaves the house followed by Max.

His parents watch from the dining room window as Craig and Max chase each other round the garden, and Craig teases Max with the ball.

Tricia and Stuart finish their lunch, and Stuart returns to the lounge and switches the TV on, and presses the remote to 3 for ITV, and then onto Teletext. He looks at the menu page, and selects page 200 for holidays, and then page 220 for the last minute bargains. There are 15 pages of adverts, starting off with the months of August, September, October, listing the resorts, or places where holidays are available on a self-catering basis. Ibiza £219, Majorca £249, Zante £239, Costa Blanca £249, Algarve 14 nights £299.

The advert states the holidays are ATOL protected and gives an 0800 number to ring.

Having frozen the page on the screen he shouts through to Tricia in the kitchen, 'What do you think to these then?'

She walks through into the lounge and sits on the settee beside him, and looks at the adverts. 'They all look good don't they,' she says.

'I think other than the Algarve they must be for a week, but it does state two weeks for the Algarve,' Stuart says. 'Well give them a ring about that one then.'

Stuart picks up the cordless phone, and rings the 0800 number on the screen. The phones ring tone is heard, and an operator answers.

'Bargain Holidays, you're through to Emma, how can I help you?'

'Hello,' Stuart replies, 'I am looking at your advert on Teletext, which is showing a two-week self-catering holiday in the Algarve in August. I was wondering if it was still available, and if you could tell me a little bit more about it?'

'Yes of course,' Emma replies, 'If you can just bear with me while I bring it up on the screen,' she says. There is a slight pause.

'Yes it's still available. It's a villa with a shared pool, and about an hours transfer time from the airport. It's at a resort called Albufeira. It's got a lovely coastline and sandy beaches nearby, and you have local restaurants and bars.'

'It sounds nice.' 'It sleeps six people in three bedrooms, and it's about 10 minutes walk from the beach,' Emma remarks.

'Just a minute, I will ask my Wife.' He puts his hand over the mouthpiece, and repeats what Emma has just said to Tricia.

'It sounds nice, go for it,' she says. Stuart removes his hand and continues the conversation with Emma.

'Yes, that sounds just what we want.' Emma then adds 'The departure date is next Saturday, is that all right?'

'Just a minute,' Stuart says. He turns to Tricia, 'The departure date is next Saturday.'

'Good God,' Tricia replies in a state of shock, 'Yes I suppose so, it doesn't give us much time, but we'll do it.'

'Yes, Ok we'll take it,' Stuart informs Emma.

'Well can I have your details please and all your families names?' Emma asks.

'Stuart, Patricia, Craig, and Claire Osborn,' he says.

'Are there any children under twelve years?' 'Yes one, Craig he's seven.'

'Your Address please?' 'Seven, Uplands Road, Fillybridge West, Worcestershire. WR six three seven QR,' Stuart replies.

'Have you any Travel Insurance?' ' No.'

'We do a Family Insurance for the two weeks for sixty pounds, would you like that?'

'Yes please.' 'Has anyone any serious disabilities or illnesses, or about to go into hospital for any treatment?'

'No,' Stuart replies. 'The total bill, including Insurance and Airport transfers and Taxes comes to £957. How would you like to pay for this?'

'With a Visa card,' and he reads out the reference numbers to Emma.

'You will be travelling from Birmingham to Faro with Air 5000, your tickets will be posted to you within the next two working days, along with your Insurance, and you depart at 7 am. Is there anything else I can help you with?'

'No, I think that covers it,' Stuart replies.

'Thank you for booking with Bargain Holidays, and I hope you have a lovely holiday.'

'Thanks,' Stuart says, and switches the phone off.

'Wow,' he says to Tricia, 'You had better start packing.' 'Yes, Yes, Yes,' she says in an excited tone, and runs into the kitchen.

18

'Craig,' she shouts, 'We're going on holiday next week.' Craig leaves his ball in the garden and runs into the house.

'What?' he says to his mother, as he puts his head round the kitchen door.

'We're going on holiday next Saturday to the Algarve.' 'Brill, can I go and tell Simon?' he asks. 'Yes if you want to.' 'Where's Algav?' he asks. 'Algarve,' Tricia corrects him. 'It's in Portugal near Spain. Don't they teach you anything in Geography?'

'Are we going on a Plane?' 'Yes, we're not walking,' 'Brill,' Craig shouts, as he rushes out of the kitchen to go and tell Simon.

Chapter 4

Having left the music shop, the two girls Claire and Sarah continue their walk through the shopping mall. They pause, and look in Clarke's shoe shop at the latest sandals and summer shoes. 'They look nice,' Claire remarks, and points to a pair of sling back sandals in white. 'I like the red ones, but, they are a bit expensive,' she remarks.

Claire looks at her watch it's a quarter to two. 'I think it's time I started to make for home,' she says to Sarah. 'OK.'

Both girls continue to walk through the shopping mall, gazing enviously into the shop windows. They pass an exclusive boutique. In the window and being displayed by a manikin, is a very attractive multi coloured bikini. 'God, that's nice,' Claire says to Sarah. 'Yes, all you need is a nice beach in Spain to wear it.'
'A fat chance of that happening,' she replies.

'I think we shall have to make a 'To Do List' to enable us to get everything sorted, so we are not in a state of panic, because I know what it's going to be like. Claire will have to sort herself out with regards to her packing,' Tricia says to Stuart.

'I'll make a start,' he says, as he finds a note pad in the dining room clutter draw, and takes a pen and walks through to the lounge, and settles down on the settee to commence the task in an orderly fashion.

'Things to do,' he writes at the top of the note pad.

He starts it off 'Find the Passports', 'Ring the Kennels', 'Suitcases from Loft', 'Currency from Thomas Cooks', 'Post Office for the E111'. 'Mow the Lawns on Friday', 'Clean the Car', 'Cancel Milk', 'Pay the Papers & cancel them', 'Washing', 'Ironing', 'First Aid Kit', 'Toilette needs', 'Sun Tan Lotion', 'Insect Bite Cream', 'Mosquito Repellent', 'Sun Hats', 'Books to read', 'Sun Glasses'.

The back gate opens, and Craig returns from telling Simon he is going on holiday.

'Right young man,' Tricia says to Craig, as he enters the kitchen
'Upstairs now.'

'Why, what have I done?' he protests. 'Nothing,' Tricia says, 'But we do need to sort out the things you are taking on holiday, and if any needs washing, so go on up to your room.' 'Great, yippee skippy,' Craig says.

She opens his wardrobe door. 'Right, what a mess. You are an untidy little devil. I only sorted this out last week.' She commences looking through the various items of clothing, selecting items which she has decided needs washing, and tidying and folding other items.

The front door opens and Claire has returned from her visit to town. 'Hi Dad,' she says as she looks into the lounge. Max bursts into the hall from the kitchen and jumps up at her. 'Hello fella,' she says, and gives him a fuss. 'Where's Mom?' Claire asks her dad, who is still studying his ' Things to do' list. 'Upstairs with Craig I think.' As she starts to climb the stairs, Craig runs from his room to the top of the stairs and shouts down to his sister.

'We're going on holiday next week to Algav,' he says.

'Oh are we, nice of someone to tell me, and to give me plenty of warning,' she says in a sarcastic tone.

'What's he babbling on about?' she says to her mother, as she follows Craig into his room.

'Your Dad has booked us a two weeks holiday in the Algarve, and we leave next Saturday.' 'Thanks for consulting me, but I might have other plans.'

'Well have you?' Tricia remarks. 'No as a matter of fact, I haven't.'

'Well what are you moaning about then?'

'But I might have,' she says. 'But you haven't, have you.' 'It's not the point.'

'So, you don't want to come then,' Tricia says. 'I didn't say that.'

'So, what are we arguing about then?' 'Just that I would have liked to have been consulted.'

'Well if you had been here you would have, but you weren't were you,' Tricia says.

'So if you can't say anything more sensible, then I would suggest you go and start to sort yourself out as to what you are likely to be taking, and let me have anything that needs washing.'

Claire storms out of Craig's room and goes to her own room.

'Girls,' Craig remarks, in a pathetic way, and smiles at his mother.

'Will I be able to have some new Trainers,' Craig asks his mother.

'We'll see,' she replies, as she continues to sift through Craig's clothes.

Having entered her bedroom, Claire reflects on her comments to her mother, and thinks to herself that she has been very unreasonable about her issue of going on holiday, but really she was quite excited. She picks her mobile phone up and rings Sarah. Ringing tone is heard, as Claire flops back and lies full length on the bed. Sarah answers her phone call. 'Hi Claire,' Sarah says, having seen Claire's name on her mobile phone display screen.

'Have a guess what?' Claire asks Sarah. 'I haven't a clue,' Sarah remarks.

'Mom and Dad have booked us on a two weeks holiday in the Algarve from next Saturday.'

'Never,' Sarah replies. ' What do you think my chances are of getting that Bikini on Monday, and those Sandals?' she asks. 'Every chance knowing you.'

'OK, but I'll have to do some grovelling,' she remarks. 'Why's that then?' Sarah asks. ' 'Cos' I've just been moaning about the fact they booked the holiday without asking me.' 'Arr you'll be all right, just offer to do the washing up for a couple of days, that usually works for me when I want something.' Both girls start laughing.

Claire's bedroom door opens, and Craig puts his head round the door to see what the laughing is about. 'What do you want, don't bother knocking then, now clear off, I am having a private conversation?'

'Err,' Craig remarks. 'Who was that?' Sarah asks. 'Craig,' Claire replies, 'Poking his nose in where it's not wanted,' she says. 'Right, where were we, oh yes, ok Monday. I'll give you a ring and let you know what's happening,' Claire says. 'Ok see you,' Sarah replies, and they switch their phones off.

Claire lies still on the bed gazing up at the ceiling slowly closing her eyes, and dreaming of wearing the bikini and being under a sun brolley reading her book on the beach. Her mind continues to drift and she slowly closes her eyes, as she gently hears the water ebbing, and flowing, and an occasional seagull cries.

'Hello my name is Sebastian, you look as if you need some sun lotion rubbed on those arms?' She looks up from her book and sees a very hansom young

Spanish boy wearing black swimming trunks. He has a soft and gentle smile as he kneels down on the burning sand beside her.

He reaches for the sun lotion, and takes the liberty to start and rub some onto her arms. 'It's very hot to-day and you must protect yourself from the sun it can do so much damage to your skin,' he says.

Claire is speechless for a few seconds as she looks into his dark brown eyes and his black curly hair. 'Oh yes, but I can do it myself,' she says in a curt and shocked manner. 'I am sure you can, but it is so much nicer when someone does it for you,' Sebastian says as he continues to rub the lotion into her skin.

'Are you here on holiday?' he asks. 'Yes,' she replies, and yet she wants him to leave her alone, but at the same time she thinks, God he is good looking, and I suppose it would be rude to send him away. 'Yes I am here with my parents and my younger brother,' she adds.

'I live just the other side of the bay with my Mother and two Sisters. My Father died two years ago.' He stops rubbing the lotion in. 'I am sorry to hear that,' she says. 'You speak very good English. I wish I spoke Spanish as well as you speak English,' Claire says, as she puts her book down and starts to concentrate on Sebastian a little more.

'I used to go to a language school in England in the Cotswolds do you know where that is.' He asks. 'Yes of course I do.' 'I was there for two years until my Father died and we came to live here in Portugal.' 'You are Spanish though?' 'Yes, but my Grandparents are Portuguese. Can I buy you a Coke only there is a nice kiosk just along the beach?' Sebastian asks Claire. 'Yes that would be nice,' as she gets up from her sun mat. 'I don't know your name?' Sebastian asks Claire. 'Claire,' she replies.

'Well Claire, I think you are very lucky to have met me.' Sebastian says. 'You mean you are very lucky to have met me.' 'Yes that is what I said.' 'Never mind,' Claire says, as she lets his bad English pass by with a smile. They walk slowly along the beach as she ties her sarong around her waist, and they chat and laugh as they walk towards the kiosk.

'Claire, Claire, Claire.' She hears her name called out several times. 'Claire are you awake?' Her mother shouts up from down stairs. 'Dinner in ten minutes.' Claire slowly opens her eyes as she still lingers in her dream of Sebastian and the beach.

Oh bother; I was enjoying that dream she thinks to herself as she slowly sits up on the bed. I wonder if I will really meet Sebastian, or someone like him on this flipping holiday.

Chapter 5

'Dinners ready,' Tricia shouts from the kitchen to anyone in the house who may be listening, as she walks through into the dining room with two plates of food, and places them at the table. She returns to the kitchen. 'It's on the table,' she shouts in a loud voice, as she seems to get the impression the house is void of people.

'There's no need to shout,' Stuart says, as he walks into the dining room from the lounge.

She picks up the remaining two meals and walks back into the dining room as Craig bounds in from the hall. 'What's for dinner Mom?' he asks. 'Suck it and see,' she replies.

'Claire, are you coming?' Tricia shouts upstairs from the hall, as Claire leaves her room and starts to descend the stairs. 'Yes, Yes, Yes, I am coming, keep your hair on.'

Tricia hears the last remark Claire made, 'Watch it Miss, or it'll end up in the bin,' Tricia scornfully remarks.

They all sit down to dinner. 'I have done the 'Things to do list',' Stuart remarks. 'Good,' Tricia replies, and they eventually finish their meals.

'What's for pud?' Craig asks his mom. 'That's all you think about, food, food, food, you are just a greedy little pig,' Claire says to Craig, as she gets up from the table. However no one takes any notice of her remarks.

'Rice Pudding, it's all I had time for to day,' Tricia replies, and at the same time giving Claire a look enough to kill.

'Yummy,' Craig says.

'Do you want some Claire?' Tricia asks, knowing full well what was coming next. 'No thanks,' she replies as she walks through into the kitchen, in order to escape any chance of a rebuttal from her mom. 'Can I do the washing up for you?' she shouts.

'Yes, of course, sure you don't want a lie down first?' Tricia says. 'Oh very funny.' Claire remarks in a sarcastic manner.

'What's up with her?' Stuart asks in a soft voice so Claire didn't hear what was said.

'I don't know,' Tricia replies, also in a soft voice trying not to be overheard.

'She has been in a mood ever since she found out we are going on holiday, and she wasn't consulted, but take no notice she'll be all right,' Tricia says.

Tricia, Stuart and Craig finish their rice puddings. Stuart gathers up the bowls in order to take them through to Claire in the kitchen.

'May I please leave the table?' Craig asks his mother. 'Yes of course,' she replies.

Claire squeezes some washing up liquid into the washing up bowl and runs the hot tap, and begins to gather up the knives and forks, and places them into the water, and makes a start on the washing up.

Stuart enters the kitchen, and places the pudding bowls onto the work surface, and reaches for a tea towel from the side of the sink unit, and begins to wipe dry the knives and forks Claire has washed. 'There's a perfectly good dishwasher there, you don't have to do this you know,' Stuart says to Claire. 'I know, I just felt like it, that's all,' she replies.

As she washes up, she looks out into the garden, and sees Max lying on the grass in the evening sun asleep. Suzy is at the top of the garden on the prowl for any birds that might fail to spot her, and she can snatch a quick meal.

'What's happening to Max and Suzy when we go away?' Claire asks her father.

'I'll book them into 'Farmhouse Kennels' for the fortnight,' he replies.

'Anyway, what's up with you?' Stuart asks Claire, who is still looking out of the window with a staring glazed look on her face, and her hands still in the washing up bowl covered in soapsuds, not really concentrating on what she is doing, as she slowly washes the dinner plates.

'Nothing.' she replies. 'Well it doesn't seem like nothing to your Mom and me. You have been really short tempered since you came back from town. Who's upset you?'

'No one. I was just thinking. Where are we going on this holiday then?' she asks.

'Portugal, and to a place called Albufeira,' Stuart replies. 'Is that by the Sea?' she asks.

'Yes, why?' Stuart replies. 'Nothing, I was just wondering.'

They are interrupted as Craig wonders in the kitchen. 'Can I have a glass of water please Dad?' Craig asks.

'No, clear off.' Claire says. 'Yes of course you can Son.' Stuart replies, as he reaches up into the cupboard to get a glass for Craig, and pours some water from the Brita's Filter jug into the glass.

He hands the lad the glass, and Craig thanks his father and returns to the lounge.

'There was no need for that remark,' Stuart says to Claire. Claire takes no notice, and continues with the washing up. Stuart finishes drying the last bowl. Claire wipes the draining board down and throws the washing up water away down the sink.

'If we are going to the Sea I shall need some new clothes,' Claire mentions in passing to her father.

'Oh yes, is that so,' he replies with a wide smile on his face, having suspected why Claire volunteered to do the washing up. Claire seizes her opportunity to get her dad, who she feels is in a good mood to agree with the request she is about to launch onto him with her feminine charms. She puts her arms around his neck and gives him a big kiss on his right cheek.

'I knew there was something fishy about you volunteering to do the washing up,' Stuart says. 'I don't know what you are talking about,' Claire replies in an impish manner.

'So what is it you want?' he asks. 'Well, I've seen this Bikini and some white Sandals.' 'Oh have you now, and how many millions of pounds are they going to cost me?' 'They are not that much,' Claire replies. 'Have you asked your Mother?' he enquires. 'No.' ' Well, we will have to see.'

They both walk through to the lounge, and join Tricia and Craig to watch the TV. Claire settles into the armchair by the window, and Stuart takes the armchair in the corner of the lounge.

'Thanks for doing the washing up you two,' Tricia says. 'OK,' Stuart replies.

Stuart relaxes in his chair, and gets really comfortable, and starts to read the paper, but falls asleep, and suddenly wakes two hours later.

'Oh you are back with us then,' Tricia remarks in a sarcastic manner.

26

'What's the time?' he asks. 'Five to Ten. Do you want a cup of Decaffeinated Tea?' Tricia asks.

'Umm I think so.' 'Do you want one Claire?' 'Please, and then I'll go to bed,' she replies.

Tricia walks into the kitchen and fills the kettle with water from the tap and switches it on.

Craig shuffles through into the kitchen half-awake, and half-asleep, and reaches up to his mother for a kiss. 'Night Max,' he says, as he makes his way upstairs to bed.

The kettle boils, and Tricia makes the tea in the white china teapot, having used two decaffeinated tea bags, and stirs the tea with a teaspoon. She lets it brew as she puts the milk in three mugs.

The tea is poured, and she takes two mugs in one hand, and one in the other, and returns to the lounge. She hands Claire her mug and gives one to Stuart. Claire kisses her parent's goodnight and goes to bed.

Shortly after Claire has left Tricia says, 'What's all the fuss with Claire?'

'Oh she asked for a Bikini and some Sandals.' 'Oh, did she now, and what did you say?' 'I asked if she had asked you, and she said she hadn't.'

'The little Madam, what if I want a Bikini?' 'You can have one if you want,' Stuart replies. 'What, with my figure.' 'Well what are you arguing about then,' 'Well,' Tricia remarks. 'Well, nothing we will have to see what tomorrow brings won't we,' Stuart replies.

Chapter 6

It's early Monday morning, and Stuart is making his early morning call to the boarding kennels.

'I've rung to see if you could board our dog and cat for two weeks from this weekend?' Stuart asks the kennel maid at Farmhouse Kennels.

'Yes we have space,' the maid replies. 'I want to bring them in on Friday, is that alright?' 'Yes, that will be fine, bring them in around 3 o'clock. Do they have any special requirements?' 'No not really. I will bring all their food and toys,' Stuart says. 'What breed are they?' the maid asks. 'Springer Spaniel and a Tortoiseshell Cat. It's Max and Suzy,' Stuart adds.

'Please pay when you arrive. It's £8 per night for the dog, and £5 for the cat. That will be £195 for 15 nights.' 'Yes OK, see you Friday,' Stuart puts the phone down.

'That's the pets sorted. Are you lot ready for town?' Stuart asks Tricia. 'Yes nearly, we are just waiting for Claire.'

Claire is on her mobile phone to Sarah. 'Well I've got to go, Mom's waiting for me, and it looks like I may get my Bikini, but I'll give you a ring when I get back, and I can show it to you.' 'Ok, see you,' Sarah says, as Claire switches off the phone.

'What are we doing, walking or going in the car?' Tricia asks. 'Walking, it's a nice day, and we could all do with the exercise,' Stuart says.

'Max,' Stuart shouts from the lounge as Max comes bounding in from the garden.

'Do you want to come?' Stuart asks the dog who is standing in front of him wagging his tail and barking. 'You do, Ok fetch your lead.' Max dashes back into the kitchen looking for his lead followed by Stuart. 'Where is it then?' Stuart asks, as the dog barks at the cupboard where the lead is kept. He opens the door, reaches in for the lead and clips it to his collar, as Max jumps up in an excited manner.

Stuart shouts upstairs to Claire and Craig, 'Are you two ready, we are off to town?'

'Coming,' Claire replies, as they both descend the stairs.

They all leave the house as Tricia locks the front door, having set the alarm. Stuart and Max take the lead as they make their way down their road, turning left at the end and walking on through the gully by the side of the park, and eventually into town.

'I am going to Thomas Cook's to get the currency. I'll see you girls in the Precinct later,' Stuart says to Tricia and Claire. 'Will you stay outside with Max?' Stuart asks Craig, as he hands him Max's lead.

Tricia and Claire continue walking towards the precinct. 'Can I have the Bikini and the Sandals then?' Claire asks her mother. 'We will see. Anyway how much are they?' Tricia asks. 'I think the Sandals were £25 and the Bikini was about the same?'

They enter the precinct, and reach the boutique where Claire had seen the bikini. It was still being displayed on the model in the window. They both stop and look at it.

'See, it is nice, and I think it will fit me?' Claire remarks.

'Ok, it does look pretty, and I think it will suit you,' Tricia says, as they both enter the shop.

Having entered Thomas Cook's, Stuart had to wait a short while as someone was being served at the Bureau de Exchange. The customer is finally served and Stuart reaches the desk.

He asks the cashier, 'Can I have eight hundred pounds in Euros please?'

'Yes, you don't mind waiting do you, only it will take a few minutes?' the cashier replies. 'No,' Stuart takes a seat, while the cashier starts to collect the various nomination of bank notes from her till, and counts them several times, to ensure the amount is correct, having checked the exchange rate for the day.

'How will you pay for them?' the cashier asks. ' With my Debit Card if that's all right?' 'Yes, that will be fine,' the cashier replies, as Stuart hands the card over to her.

She swipes the card through the till machine, and waits a short while, as the transaction is verified, and the till roll is ejected from the machine. The cashier tears off the slip and hands it to Stuart to sign.

'Would you like the Currency in a folder?' she asks. 'Yes please.' The cashier bags the money and hands it to Stuart.

'Going anywhere nice?' she asks. 'Yes Portugal.' 'Oh I've been there, we stayed at Albufeira.' 'That's where we are going,' Stuart replies.

'You'll like it there, it's a lovely place.' 'I hope so.' Stuart thanks the cashier and leaves the shop.

'Now we have to go to the Post Office,' Stuart says to Craig, who has been waiting patiently outside the travel agents.

Stuart takes Max's lead and they walk on down to the post office, which is situated just off the high street. Stuart hands Craig the dog's lead again as he enters the post office.

He looks to his right, and finds the information board that contains various forms and booklets. He finds the E111 holiday booklet, he takes it from the rack, and walks over to the customers writing counter, and starts to fill in the form.

Having completed the form, he takes it to the post office cashier, and hands it over. The assistant checks the form to ensure it has been completed correctly, and stamps it with the post office date stamp. She tears off her portion, and hands the remaining booklet and form back to Stuart. 'Thank you,' he says.

He leaves the post office and rejoins Craig and Max. 'Right, now we have to go and meet your Mother.' He reaches for Max's lead and they start to make their way towards the precinct.

'Dog's are not allowed in the Precinct,' Stuart says to Craig, 'So wait here a minute while I go and find your Mother, I think she will be just inside.'

Stuart begins to walk inside the precinct, when he sees Tricia and Claire leaving the boutique, having purchased her bikini. Stuart makes his way towards them, and as he reaches them he says to Tricia. 'Craig is waiting outside with the dog, I'll send him to you and you can get him those Trainers he's been on about.'

Stuart returns to Craig. 'Your Mothers waiting over there for you, so go with her and Claire they'll get you those Trainers you've been on about.' 'Cheers Dad,' and Craig runs towards his mother.

The three of them walk further up the crowded precinct to Clarke's shoe shop, where they are displaying several pairs of sports trainers, and ladies sandals in the window.

They enter the shop, and look at several pairs of trainers. Craig spots a pair with blue flashes on both sides, and reflectors in the heel.

'I like these Mom,' he says, as he reaches to get the one on display from the shelf.

'How much are they?' she asks him, as he looks under the sole at the price tag. 'Twenty four pounds,' he says. 'God, they are dear, can't you find anything cheaper?' 'They are cheap,' Claire says, 'You can pay sixty, or seventy pounds for a pair,' she adds.

Claire spots her white sandals on the ladies display shelf, and takes the display shoe down. 'These are the Sandals I've been on about,' she says to her mother, as she hands it to her for her to look at.

'They're nice, and how much are these?' 'Oh twenty-eight pounds,' she says, answering her own question, as she sees the price label on the underside of the sandal.

'Give them here. I'll ask if they have your sizes.' She walks over to the assistant. 'Have you got these Trainers in a Childs Size 7, and the Sandal in a Size 5, please?' she asks. 'Just a minute, I'll check in the Stockroom,' the assistant replies, as she walks off down the back of the shop.

After a short while, the assistant returns with a pair of trainers and sandals.

'We have them in your sizes,' she says as she hands them over to Tricia, for Craig and Claire to try on.

Tricia sits Craig on the chair and kneels down in front of him, unties and removes the shoes he is currently wearing, fits one of the new trainers on his foot, threads the laces through the lace holes and ties the shoe up. 'How's that feel?' she asks Craig.

'Ok,' he replies, as Tricia fits the new trainer on his other foot, threading the laces and tying the shoe up. 'Have a walk in them,' she says to Craig, who gets off the chair and walks slowly round the shop.

'How do they feel?' she asks. 'Ok,' he says. 'What about your toes, is there plenty of room?' 'Yes.' 'Does your heel pull out?' 'No,' he replies.

'They look good Mom,' Claire says, as Craig walks back and sits down. 'Are you sure they are Ok?' 'Yes they're fine,' Craig replies.

Tricia starts to remove the trainers, puts them in the box, and Craig puts his old shoes back on.

31

Claire has put the sandals on, and starts to walk round the shop. 'What do you think Mom?' she asks. 'They look Ok, do they feel all right?'

'Yes, they are very comfortable.' Claire sits down, removes the sandals, and places them back in the box.

'We will have them,' Tricia says to the assistant, and hands them to her.

'That will be fifty two pounds,' the assistant says, as Tricia hands over her debit card. The assistant gives Tricia the till receipt, which she places into one of the carrier bags. 'Thanks,' Tricia says, and they leave the shop.

'Where to next?' Claire asks her mother. 'Boots the Chemists for some Sun Tan Lotion, but we had better find your Dad.'

They all walk outside the precinct and find Stuart and Max sitting on a bench in the sun. Max sits up and jumps up to Craig as he joins his Dad on the bench. 'Hello Max,' says Craig, as he gives the dog some fuss. 'How have you got on?' Stuart asks.

'Ok, Claire's got her Bikini and Sandals, they are very nice, and I've just bought Craig his Trainers. We're just going to Boots for some Sun Tan lotion, are you staying with your Dad?' Tricia asks Craig 'Yes,' he says.

'Do you want to see my new Trainers?' Craig asks his dad. 'Yes,' Stuart says, as Craig starts to get the box out of the carrier bag with Max sniffing at it hoping it is some food. 'Gosh, they are posh,' his dad says.

Tricia and Claire walk off in the direction of Boots in the high street. They enter the shop and Claire picks up a basket inside the doorway, and they start looking for the cosmetics and suntan lotions. The range of lotions is vast, with different makes and suntan ratings, which requires considerable studying as to their personal requirements.

'What factor should we have?' Tricia asks Claire. 'I think factor thirty should be Ok for us all don't you?' she says, as she picks a bottle of Ambre Solaire up off the display shelf.

'It says sun block milk, which will rub in easy, and its suitable for children and sensitive skins. It's also anti Uva/Uvb, and water-resistant, and anti ageing.'

'Ok, we will have some of that, and its buy one and get one free, so we should have enough for us all for the holiday. I think we should have some after sun lotion as well.'

They both look a little further along the shelving, and find the after sun lotion. Tricia picks a Nivea bottle up, and reads the label on the front, which says moisturising after sun lotion with vitamin E.

'I think this will be Ok, it cools the skin after you have been sun bathing,' she says.

'Now is there anything else we want?' Tricia asks Claire. 'What about mosquito repellent tablets, and insect bite cream?' 'Oh yes, we want some of those.'

They start to wonder round the shop, but can't find them. 'I don't know where they are. Do you?' Tricia asks Claire. 'No, let's ask an Assistant.' Claire spots an assistant stacking shelves, and she walks over to her. 'Excuse me, I am looking for mosquito repellent tablets, and insect bite cream, I wonder if you could show me where they are?' she asks.

'Yes of course. They are over there next to the first aid kits.' 'Oh thank you,' Claire says, as she makes her way further round the display shelves towards them.

'Here they are,' she says to her mother. Tricia picks them up and puts them in her shopping basket. 'I think we should have some plasters?' Claire says ' You can if you like, but we do have a First Aid Kit at home, which is fully stocked.' 'Ok, I'll leave it then.'

'What's next?' Claire asks. 'Travel sick pills, you know what Craig's like,' Tricia says.

'You'll have to get them off the Pharmacy counter,' Claire says to her mother.

'Right that's it then. I'll go and pay for this lot, and get the travel sick pills,' Tricia says, as she makes her way over to the pharmacy counter.

She joins a short queue and waits her turn. Eventually she gets to the counter and places her basket on it for the assistant to price up the items. 'Can I also have some travel sickness pills?' she asks.
' Yes, a box of twelve, or twenty four?' 'Oh twelve please,' Tricia replies.

Tricia pays for the items, and they return to Stuart and Craig outside, and make their way home.

Chapter 7

Stuart switches the radio on in the dining room, just as the radio stations 8 o'clock news begins and the announcer says, 'This is the International and Regional news, and weather forecast for Tuesday 7th August.' The announcer continues with his broadcast, but Stuart's mind is on other things, as he still has to find the passports, and get the suitcases out of the loft after everyone has had breakfast.

The sun is shining, and he takes the mug of tea he'd just made outside, and sits on the garden bench, and although he had not long woken up, he settles into a relaxed mood in the early morning sunshine.

Max wonders round the garden taking in the morning air. He hears the letterbox slap shut, as the morning newspaper is pushed through by the papergirl. He dashes in, grabs the paper, and returns outside to Stuart, and gives it to him. 'Thanks, that's a good boy,' Stuart says, as he takes the paper from Max, and pats him on his head.

Stuart unfolds the paper and looks at the headlines, and thinks more doom and gloom. I don't know why I bother he thinks to himself, as he turns over the pages reading the headlines of each story.

His thoughts direct him to thinking the adverts are more interesting than the news items. Why they can't put stories in of happier events beats me.

He looks up into the sky, and sees a white vapour trail of a jet passing overhead as it heads south. I bet they're off on holiday lucky devils, but we will be up there in a couple of days he thinks, as he sees the jet pass out of sight.

He hears the kitchen door open, and he turns round to see Tricia has come downstairs in her dressing gown for breakfast. She walks outside. 'Hi love, its lovely and warm,' as she sits down beside Stuart on the bench, and cuddles up to him. They both appreciate the early morning warm sunshine, and the peace and quiet of the lovely summer morning. Stuart offers her a sip of his tea, which she takes. 'Thanks,' she says, and hands him back the mug.

Then they both hear the kitchen door bang open. 'Give me that back. I'll belt you one,' Claire shouts in a loud voice, as Craig runs out of the house followed by Claire. Their peace is shattered.

'That's the peace over,' Stuart says. 'What's the matter with you two?' Tricia asks, as Craig runs up the garden swinging Claire's bikini top round, and giggling at the same time.

Claire chases after him, but she's not amused, as Craig lets go of it, and drops it onto the grass. 'I'll get you for this,' she says. She bends down and picks it up. 'Look what he's done, he's ruined it,' she protests.

'I am sure he hasn't. Behave yourselves, and come and have some breakfast,' Tricia says, as Stuart and Tricia get up from the bench, and make their way back into the house.

'I am not eating with him,' Claire remarks in an angry tone, and as her mother's back is turned she manages to clip Craig round the ear with her hand. He promptly starts crying, and runs through into the lounge. 'Now what have you done?' Tricia shouts at Claire. 'Nothing, I never touched him,' Claire protests her innocence at the accusations her mother cast upon her.

'He's crying. He doesn't cry for nothing. Now what did you do?' Tricia sternfully asks. Craig shouts from the lounge, 'She hit me.' 'Well I might have touched him, but he deserved it. He should have more respect for other people's property,' Claire says.

'I dare say, but he is your younger Brother. Now go and say sorry.'
'No way, I am not apologising to him, until he apologises to me first,' Claire says. 'Craig say sorry,' Tricia shouts to Craig.

'No,' he shouts back from the lounge. 'Well there's no breakfast. I mean it, and you can forget about going on holiday. It's not too late to cancel it,' Tricia says.

The sobbing slowly subsides, and a very faint 'Sorry' can be heard coming from Craig in the lounge. 'What was that,' Tricia said. 'Sorry,' Craig replied in a little louder tone. 'That's better,' Tricia replied. 'Now you Claire,' Tricia said. ' I don't see why I should, he started it in the first place.' Tricia made no reply, but looked scornfully at her. 'Oh all right. Sorry, does that satisfy you,' Claire says to her mom. 'Don't be such a cheeky madam.'

'Now lets have breakfast in peace please,' Tricia says, as she helps Stuart lay the table. 'Get the cutlery out, will you please,' she says to Claire, and they eventually have a peaceful meal without further incident.

Having had his shower, Stuart makes a start on finding the passports. I am sure I last saw them in the bedside draws he thinks to himself, as he sifts through the old birthday cards and various items of memorabilia, including old photos of the kids when they were babies. He comes across an envelope containing all their birth and marriage certificates, but still no sign of the passports.

He opens the next draw down, which appears to be full of make up bottles of Tricia's, and tights and knitting patterns. He gives up on that draw as a total dead loss.

His final hopes are pinned on the last draw, where he finds some old flight magazines he had forgotten about, and begins to read them.

After several minutes of looking through the magazines, he decides he had better continue with his search. Under various other pieces of papers and old letters, he finally finds what he has been searching for. The passports were inside an old brown envelope marked 'Passports.'

'Got'ya,' he says to himself, as he removes it from the draw and opens it up. 'There they are,' he says, as he reaches in and pulls them out. The first one he opens is Claire's, and he checks the date is Ok, which it is. Then the next one is his, and that is Ok for dates, and so are the other two.

He takes a long look at his own passport photograph, which really makes him look so young compared with how he looks today. Craig was only a young lad of four when his first passport photo was taken and he looks nothing like that now.

He looks at Tricia's photo in her passport, and thinks blimey her hair wasn't half long.

He thinks to himself that passport photographs don't half make you look ancient. How on earth the immigration people ever see the photograph as resembling you beats me. He puts them back in the envelope, and tidies up the draw.

Now for the suitcases he says to himself, as he heads for the landing and reaches for the loft trap door opening pole from inside the airing cupboard.

He looks up at the loft hatch situated on the landing by the airing cupboard, and puts the pole into the latch release, he pulls the latch, the door swings open down towards him.

He then uses the pole to pull the loft ladder down. 'Can I go up there Dad?' Craig asks. 'No, now get out of the way,' he says.

'What are you going up there for?' Craig asks. 'I am getting the Suitcases for the holiday,' Stuart replies, as he starts to climb the ladder. His head pokes through into the loft area he reaches in, and switches the lofts light on to find the suitcases.

He looks to his left and sees them stacked on top of one another. There are four all told, and he grabs the first one, which is slightly smaller than the others, and starts to make his way back down the ladder, and places it on the landing. He climbs up again, and gets the others.

Having completed his task, he switches off the light, and pushes the ladder back into the loft, locking the door.

The smaller suitcase is Craig's and the others will be used between Claire, Tricia, and himself.

He takes one of the cases, and places it in Claire's room. 'There's your Suitcase Claire. You can start packing when you like now,' he says to her.

He leaves the small one by Craig's bedroom door, and he takes the others through into his own bedroom.

'Ah you've got the Suitcases down,' Tricia says, as she climbs the stairs and reaches the landing, as Stuart enters their bedroom with theirs. 'Thanks that will be a help. I'll be able to start packing when I want,' she says. 'Claire you can do your own packing,' she shouts, but there is no reply, due to the fact she has her Hi Fi on, and the music thumps out its beat right through the house.

'Turn that row down,' Stuart shouts at the top of his voice. 'Sorry,' Claire says, and turns the volume down.

Tricia spots the brown envelope containing the passports lying on the bed and picks it up. 'You found them then,' she says to Stuart 'Yes, they were in the bottom draw under some papers.' 'Let's have a look and see what I look like,' she says, as she opens the envelope and removes all the passports, and sifts through them, until she finds her own. She opens it, and looks at her photo. 'Oh my God, just look at me, don't I look awful?' she says, as she falls back on the bed laughing. 'I can't believe I had my hair that long. God you can't let anyone see this.'

'You want to see mine then,' Stuart says. Tricia looks through the other passports and finds Craig's. 'Ah, doesn't he look lovely with his blonde hair.' She continues searching until she finds Stuart's passport. 'Oh my God, I can't believe this is you. You have changed haven't you,' and she starts to laugh.

Craig enters the room and sits on the bed next to his mother. 'Have I got one of those?' he asks, 'Yes, here's yours.' Tricia hands him his passport. 'Is that me?' he asks, looking at his photograph in the passport, 'Yes, that's my baby boy,' Tricia replies in a teasing manner. Craig doesn't quite know what to make of it.

Then he finds Claire's passport and opens it up. 'Is this Claire?' he asks. 'Yes,' Tricia replies. He runs into Claire's room, 'I've got your Passport you look a real nerd,' he says. 'Give it here you little sod.' Craig runs out of her room and back to his mother's room and dives on the bed. 'Now, now, you two, not again,' Tricia says in a loud voice.

'He's got my Passport and won't give it back, give it here,' Claire says, 'Give it back and stop messing about Craig,' Tricia says, as she grabs his leg and pulls him back along the bed.

Craig realises he is out numbered, and has no means of escape. So he reluctantly surrenders the passport to his mother.

Claire holds her hand out, and her mother hands it to her. She opens it up, looks at her photo, but makes no comment, hands it back to her mother, and returns to her room in disgust.

Having promised Sarah a look at her new bikini and sandals, she decides to ring her on her mobile phone.

Sarah answers the phone. 'Hi it's me,' Claire says. 'I was just washing my hair,' Sarah replies, 'Oh, sorry, I was wondering if you wanted to see the Bikini I bought yesterday.' 'Yes, I'll come round in half an hour.' 'Ok,' Claire replies, and switches off her phone.

Claire returns to her parent's bedroom and stands in the doorway. 'Sarah's coming round in half an hour to see my Bikini,' she says to her mother. 'Ok,' Tricia replies.

'I think I ought to clean these Suitcases,' Stuart says to Tricia. He picks up their suitcases and takes them downstairs to the kitchen, gets a damp floor cloth and wipes them all over. That look's better he thinks to himself as he returns upstairs, and brings the other two suitcases down, and gives them a good clean.

The front door bell rings, he leaves the cases, and answers it, fighting Max back at the same time. He opens the door and Sarah is standing there. 'Oh hello Sarah, come on in.' She steps inside the hall and makes a fuss of Max. 'Claire's upstairs in her room, just follow the music,' he says, and they both smile as she starts to climb the stairs.

Stuart returns to the kitchen and continues cleaning the suitcases. Tricia leaves the bedroom as Sarah reaches the top of the stairs.

'Hello Mrs Osborn,' 'Hello Sarah, how's your Mom and Dad, I haven't seen them in ages?' 'Ok, but they have been busy with the shop, and they never seem to have a minute these days.' 'Never mind, remember me to them. Claire's in there.' 'Yes I will,' Sarah says, as she turns towards Claire's room. 'Hi, come in and shut the door,' Claire says, and Sarah closes the door behind her. ' We want to keep Craig out, the nosy little devil,' they both laugh.

Claire takes the bikini out of her suitcase and lays it on the bed. 'What do you think?' Claire asks Sarah. 'God it's brill isn't it.' 'Yes I think so, and I managed to get my sandals as well.' 'You crafty devil,' Sarah replies. 'I had to do the washing up, but like you said, it worked.' They both fall onto Claire's bed giggling.

Chapter 8

On Wednesday afternoon's, Tricia usually visits her mother in a residential home for the elderly, which normally requires her taking two buses to the other side of town, as Stuart usually has the car for work. However, as Stuart is around she rather hoped he might take her.

Having pulled his golfing trolley out of the shed, Stuart makes a start on giving it a clean, and he is standing outside the shed when Tricia joins him.

'I am going to see Mom this afternoon, but as you are around would you give me a lift?' Tricia asks Stuart. 'I am playing Golf this morning with Dave, but I'll be back for lunch, and I don't see why not, I haven't seen her for a while,' he replies. 'Thanks, I'll see if the kids will come.'

Stuart carries on cleaning his golf clubs and sorting them out, as Tricia enters the house and goes upstairs to ask if Claire and Craig would like to see their grandma later in the day.

Having cleaned his golf trolley, Stuart loads his golf bag and trolley into the back of his white Range Rover. Although it's a fairly old vehicle it is in excellent condition. As his fetish love affair with Range Rovers ensures he keeps the vehicle well preserved, despite the expensive running costs, but due to the fact he does very little mileage in it, he is able to afford to run it.

Stuart returns to the house via the kitchen to collect his golfing shoes from the cupboard under the stairs. He shouts to Tricia upstairs. 'I am off now. I'll see you later.'

Tricia replies 'Don't be late, you know I want to see Mom this afternoon.'

Stuart closes the front door as he leaves the house, throws his golf shoes in the back of the Range Rover, and closes the tailgate. He gets in the driver's seat, puts his seat belt on, starts the engine, and reverses out of the driveway.

He slowly drives down the road, turns left at the bottom of the road, and stops outside Dave's house; he is ready and waiting for him.

'Morning Dave,' Stuart says, as he gets out of the car. 'It's a nice morning for it.' Stuart helps Dave load his trolley into the back of the Range Rover.' Yes we should have a good game.' Stuart closes the tailgate, they both get in, and they make their way to the golf course.

Meanwhile back at home, bang, the letterbox slams shut, and letters are heard to fall onto the hall carpet. Max hears the noise and makes a dash into the hall; he grabs one of the envelopes, and starts to chew at it. 'Max leave it alone,' Tricia shouts from the top of the stairs in a loud voice. Max looks up at her and thinks about what has been said to him, and stands wagging his tail with it still in his mouth. Tricia comes down the stairs in order to get the letter before Max completely destroys it.

'Good-boy give it here,' Tricia says, as she reaches down and retrieves the letter from him, and gives him a pat on the head. She then picks up the remaining letters.

Tricia walks into the kitchen and starts to open the letters one by one; there are three all together. The first two, including the one Max was chewing are junk mail, but the third letter looks very thick, she opens it, and finds it's from the travel company, and the flight tickets have arrived for the holiday.

She starts to check through them, and finds they are all in order with their correct names. The tickets state the flight is due to depart at seven am Saturday 11th August, departing Birmingham to Faro, and check - in time two hours before the flight.

God, we will have to be up early that morning, Tricia thinks to herself. If we have to be checked in by five am, we will have to be there before four thirty, and it takes an hour to travel there, so we must leave by three thirty, and we shall have to be up by three. God, it's hardly worth going to bed in the first place, she thinks.

'The tickets have arrived,' she shouts in a loud voice up the stairs to Claire and Craig. Craig is heard to run down the stairs still in his pyjamas, 'Can I see them?' he asks as he reaches the kitchen. Tricia shows him the tickets, 'Nosy, there is nothing to see,' she says.

'Have I got one?' he asks. 'Yes this is yours,' as Tricia finds his ticket in with the others. 'Now go on upstairs, get washed, and dressed, and tell Claire to do the same,' Tricia says to Craig, as he runs back upstairs, and shouts to Claire 'The tickets have come, and Mom said get washed and dressed.'

Stuart pulls up on the car park of the golf course, and they both begin to unload their golfing trolleys, and put on their golfing shoes.

'The last time I played here was about two weeks ago, and the greens were not up to scratch. I hope they have improved things since then,' Stuart says to Dave, who is tying his laces up. 'They had last week when I came,' he replies. 'I shall have to watch the time I'm afraid today, as Tricia wants to see her Mom this afternoon,' Stuart says to Dave.

'Shall we have nine holes then?' Dave asks. 'Yes, that's Ok with me,' Stuart says, as they both make their way towards the golf house to pay for the round.

They leave their trolleys outside the golf house, and go in to pay for their round of nine holes. Having paid, and walked to the first tee Stuart says, 'Shall I go first?' 'If you like,' replies Dave.

Stuart reaches into his golf bag, which is attached to his golf trolley, selects a number five-pinseeker wood, and a tee pin, and places his golf ball on the tee, having selected the spot he wishes to drive from.

He takes a few practise swings to loosen his arms and back, and then settles down to take his shot. Other than an odd bird noise, all is quiet as he concentrates on his stance. He looks towards the pin of the first hole, which is a par 4 425-yard up hill shot, with mature oak trees on the left, and elm trees on the right.

Stuart makes his shot, the ball flies high and long, and lands slightly to the left of the centre line of the fairway, three or four yards short of the rough dried grass, and about 120 yards away. He is very pleased with his shot as he bends down to retrieve his tee.

Dave also selects a number five wood from his golf bag, along with a bright yellow golf ball, and a yellow tee pin. He places his tee in the soft grass he'd selected to drive from, and pushes it in, and places his ball onto the tee pin.

Like Stuart he takes a few practise swings, and then hits the ball. The ball flies low, swings violently to the left, hits an oak tree, and bounces off and lands in the rough grass. 'Bloody hell, what happened with that?' Dave asks Stuart, as he bends down to retrieve his tee pin. 'I think you may well have clipped the top of the ball,' Stuart replies, as they make their way with their trolleys towards their respective balls along the fairway.

The children have all had their washes, and Tricia starts to clean the bathroom when the doorbell rings. Craig shouts, 'I'll get it,' as he rushes down the stairs followed by Max, who almost knocks him over as he goes by. Craig reaches the front door and opens it to find his Auntie Katrina and Cousin Kate standing there.

Although Katrina is younger than her sister Tricia by 12 months, and works full time with her husband Steve in the family building business, she is petite in stature, with dark black hair, and slim figure. Kate is her 17-year-old daughter, who has a vain nature, and insists on nothing but the best in life, and is very tall and mature for her age.

'Hello Craig, is your Mom in?' Katrina asks. Tricia shouts from upstairs, ' Who is it?' 'It's Auntie Katrina,' he replies, and at the same time invites them in.

'Well let her in,' Tricia shouts, 'I won't be a minute, I am in the bathroom.' Katrina fusses Max and they all enter the lounge.

'Is Claire in?' Kate asks Craig. 'She's upstairs in her room, do you want to go and see her?' 'Please,' Kate replies, and she makes her way upstairs to see her cousin Claire.

'We're going on holiday on Saturday,' Craig tells Katrina. 'Oh that will be nice, where are you going?' 'To Algav, and we're going on a plane,' he adds, as he lolls on the settee. 'That sounds great. Have you packed yet?' 'No, but I have my own case.'

With that Tricia enters the lounge as Craig makes a break for his room upstairs, 'Sorry about that, I was just cleaning the bathroom,' she says, as she leans down to give her sister a kiss.

'That's all right, we were just passing on our way to town, to do some shopping. Craig tells me you are going on holiday on Saturday.' 'Yes, one of those last minute jobs. We're going to the Algarve in Portugal self catering, but it should be nice. Do you want a coffee?' 'Yes please,' Katrina says, as Tricia leaves the lounge and enters the kitchen.

'Stuart's gone golfing this morning, but he will be back for lunch as he's taking me to see Mom this afternoon,' Tricia says, as she starts to fill the kettle with water, and gets two mugs down from the overhead kitchen cupboard. 'It's the only time I have at the moment to see her before we go. We have to be at the Airport at five am on Saturday, but we are flying from Birmingham so it shouldn't be too bad.'

'I saw Mom last week, and she seemed fine,' Katrina remarks.

The kettle boils and Tricia pours the hot water into the mugs, and the coffee dissolves as the hot water hits the granules, she then adds the milk. 'Shall we have the coffee in the garden?' Tricia asks Katrina. 'Coming,' she replies, and they both walk into the garden to enjoy the warm morning sunshine, and to catch up on family news. Tricia places the tray and the two coffee mugs down on the white wrought iron garden table, with its brightly coloured sun brolley to give some shade.

'How's Steve?' Tricia asks. 'Well, much the same as usual.' They both sip their coffee. 'The truth is things haven't been going too well just lately.' 'Oh,' Tricia says.

They take another sip of coffee and Tricia wafts a wasp away, and waits quietly for Katrina to speak again.

'I went to town a few weeks ago, and called into the Majestic Hotel down by the river for lunch. I was having a glass of wine and reading a magazine I had bought. There were several businessmen sitting the other side of the room having a drink, and I wasn't particularly taking any notice of them. One of them got up from their table to go to the bar, and as he passed by, he caught the chair at my table and knocked it over, knocking my shopping all over the floor. He said he was sorry and helped me to gather the things up. I said it was all right, but he apologised even more, and asked if he could buy me a drink for the trouble he had caused. I said, no thank you, I was going soon. He apologised again, and went to the bar to get the drinks for his guests, shortly afterwards I left.'

Katrina sips some more of her coffee. 'Dam wasps,' Tricia says, as she wafts another one away.

Katrina continues her conversation of the events in a quiet tone of voice. 'About two weeks later, I went back to the Majestic for afternoon tea, and who should be in there but that chap I had seen two weeks previously. He came across and asked if I was Ok, and he was pleased to see me again. He introduced himself, and said his name was Alex, and he was a Pharmaceutical Rep, and he visited the town every two weeks or so. We chatted about ordinary things, and he bought me a glass of red wine, and we chatted even more. He was staying at the Majestic, as he lived in London, and usually stayed there for a couple of nights when he was in town. He seemed very nice and was well mannered, very tall and slim, with dark black hair, and was wearing a light grey suit, with a white shirt and pin-striped tie, he looked very smart. He told me he wasn't married or attached. Not that I was interested anyway,' Katrina said, 'No' Tricia replied.

'Anyway I had a sip of wine, and put it back down on the table, but I don't know what happened, I must have missed the mat as the glass fell over and the wine went all over the table and down my dress. Oh God, I said as I stood up, and tried to wipe it off. He said don't worry, come up to my room and I will try and clean it. I don't know why I agreed to go, I must have been mad, but I went anyway.

He got a shower sponge and wet it, and started to rub the mark of the wine off, but the dress got wetter, and he put some soap on it and wet it again, and it did seem to come off. He then dried it with the hair drier in the room. By now I was feeling hot in more ways than one. I was thinking God he is good looking, and I was feeling uncomfortable with the situation, and thought I had better get out ASAP. Then he said the dress is still a little damp, would you like a coffee until it dries completely. I said no, I had better get back, but then I really wanted to

44

stay. I looked out of his window and the view over the river was lovely. I said you have a lovely view from your room, and he came closer to the window, and closer to me.

By now he was very close and I found myself looking up into his dark brown longing eyes, he smiled gently, and my heart started to beat quicker. I said to myself, God he is good looking. Then I thought now come on, get to grips with yourself girl, this is getting out of hand, you have got to get out of here and fast. He lent down slowly as if to kiss me and stopped, then he came closer and I closed my eyes and stopped breathing. He touched my hand and I froze with a schoolgirl nervous anticipation.

We kissed, something said this is wrong, but something else said God this is lovely.

Then his room phone rang, and we stopped. By now I was very hot, and flushed. I said I think you had better answer it. The phone rang again and again. He moved away towards the dressing table and answered the phone. Yes Ok, I'll be down in a minute he said, and replaced the receiver.

I said I think I had better go, don't you. I then made a start for the door. He blocked my way, but in a nice way, and asked if he could see me again. I said I think we have gone far enough. He said I am not sorry for what I did, and I would like to see you again. I said we'd have to see. I opened the door and left.

I couldn't sleep that night, or for the next few nights, and I just couldn't stop thinking about him. I found myself gazing out of the kitchen window, doing the washing up, and washing the same plate for ages.'

'My, you have got it bad,' Tricia said. 'I know, and it should have stopped there, but it didn't.

Two weeks later I was shopping in Selfridges and was looking at some perfume. I sprayed some on my wrist and it smelt very nice, so I decided to buy it. I reached into my handbag and removed my purse. I took out a £20 note, but before I could hand it to the assistant, an arm passed over my shoulder with a £20 note in it, and a voice from behind said we'll take it, I looked round and it was Alex.

Hello, he said. I said thank you, but you shouldn't. He said I should, because I would need it if we were to have dinner tonight at his Hotel.'

'Oh my God,' Tricia said. 'Yes, that's what I thought. The Assistant handed me the perfume, and we started to walk out of the shop together. Somehow I felt safe, and comfortable with him. He said have you got time for a coffee, I said yes, and we walked across the road into the Café Rouge. He ordered two coffees' and we chatted for ages. He said well, what about this dinner tonight. I said I can't, I have a family to think about, but I must admit the temptation was really pulling. I thought Wednesday nights is usually my Yoga class, so if I got back, did their tea, and made a dash for it, I could do it.

I said Ok. Then I thought I must be mad, but I will have to go now and I'll see you about seven. Seven it is then, he said, as I left the table and made my way out. He didn't follow me. I went to the Car Park to get my car, and I couldn't remember which floor it was on. I did eventually find it and got home, how I don't know. I don't remember passing any traffic lights or going round any roundabouts.

Tea was a very hurried affair, and I had to make myself look smart, but without going over the top. I picked up my Rucksack with my Leotard in, and said to Steve can you do the washing up, I am off to my Yoga class. I gave him a kiss, and he said he would. I said I might be a bit late back, Pat has asked me to go for a drink afterwards it's her Birthday. Don't wait up, but it might be about eleven when I get in.'

They both sipped some more coffee. Tricia said, 'It's cold, shall I do another one?' 'Please,' Katrina replied.

Tricia went into the house and made another cup of coffee. Katrina got up and started to walk around the garden, looking at the flowers. Max was lying in the sun half-asleep, and Katrina bent down and stroked him. He didn't move for a minute, then he rolled over onto his back to have his tummy rubbed. 'You are an old fusspot aren't you,' she said as she gave him a rub.

Katrina heard Tricia come back and place the coffees on the table, and so she returned to have her coffee.

'So how was Dinner then?' Tricia asked. 'Oh I think it was all right, I don't remember much about it really. We talked, and talked, and talked, he told me all about his life. How his parents had split up, and he had two Sisters and a Brother. How he became a Rep and he had a passion for fast cars, owned a Morgan Sports Car, and enjoyed long drives in the summer with the top down, liked eating out and going to the Theatre. The waiter asked if we would like coffee. He looked at me, and somehow he must have read my mind. He said no thank you. Then he said, would you like coffee in my room? I said yes.

We left the dining room and made our way to his room. He put the kettle on and put some coffee into the cups, as I looked out of his window again over the river.

He came to the window and put his hand on my shoulder, I looked into his eyes and my heart started to race again. We kissed, I heard the kettle click off and we fell gently back onto the bed. By now I was that schoolgirl again and I felt safe, and we made love, and it was wonderful. It was as if I was in a dream, yet I knew things felt right. He stroked my hair, kissed my forehead and I felt cold. I reached for the cover, he pulled it over my naked body and we held each other tight. I didn't want the night to end. I said what's the time, he looked at his watch, it's a quarter to eleven. Oh my God I said, I'd better go. I leapt out of bed and grabbed my clothes, went to the bathroom and started to get dressed. I combed my hair. He knocked on the bathroom door and opened it slowly and handed me my shoes. He said must you go. Yes I must. Will I see you again he asked. I said I don't know. Can I ring you, God no I said, as I put some Lipstick on. No, I know where you are, and I want to keep it that way. I made my way to the door and he was standing there naked. Just one more kiss he said. I said yes Ok, then I must go. I gave him one quick kiss. He said that was awful, can't a dying man have a better one than that. No I said. Arrh he said, looking at me with his soulful eyes. No, now get out of the way, I am about to open the door and someone might see you. He said I don't care. I said well I do, now shift. I opened the door and he stood behind it as I left.'

'Have you seen him since?' Tricia asked. 'No, and it's been two months now. I have managed to steer well clear of the Majestic and Selfridges, but I still think about him, may be one day I might just pluck up the courage again. I wouldn't want this to go any further you know.' 'I know,' Tricia says.

'I am worried about Kate and her exam results, I do hope she does well, she has worked hard in the last twelve months and we are hoping she will get to University,' Katrina says to Tricia. 'I am sure she will. Does she still want to be a Doctor?' 'Very much so, I don't know what will happen if she doesn't get the grades she hopes to get.' 'She's a sensible girl,' Tricia replies.

'What about Claire?' Katrina asks. ' Well, we won't know how she's got on until we get back off holiday.'

Stuart and Dave have finished their game of golf and make their way back to Stuarts Range Rover. 'Thanks for the game it was great, but I think I shall have to practise my putting,' Stuart says to Dave. 'And I think I had better put a few more hours down the driving range, or get some new clubs,' Dave remarks, as they load their golfing trolley's into the back of Stuart's Range Rover and make their way home.

Katrina finishes her coffee. 'Well we had better get off,' she says as she gets up and starts to make her way into the house. 'Kate, come on we are going now,' Katrina shouts upstairs to her daughter.

'We will keep our fingers crossed for her,' Tricia says, as Kate comes down the stairs followed by Claire.

'Thanks for the chat,' Kate says to Claire and gives her Auntie Tricia a kiss.

'Good luck with your exam results,' Tricia says to Kate. 'Thanks Auntie Tricia.' They all step outside to wave them off just as Stuart returns. He stops his Range Rover on the drive and gets out. 'Oh, you're just going then?' Stuart asks. 'I am afraid so, have a great holiday and send us a card,' Katrina says, as she gets into her car.

'How did it go then?' Tricia asks Stuart, who has just opened the tailgate on the Range Rover, and begins to remove his golf clubs. 'Not too bad, I just beat Dave by two strokes in the end, but my putting was hopeless.' 'Well come on then we will have some lunch,' Tricia says.

Chapter 9

The family have had their lunch, and Tricia returns to the kitchen after cutting some flowers from the garden for her mother. 'I think Mom will like these, Sweet-peas are her favourite flower and they smell really nice, it's a pity she can't smell them,' Tricia says to Stuart.

'Come on you two,' Stuart shouts upstairs to Craig and Claire, 'We're off to see your Nan.'

Tricia wraps the flowers in foil as the two children leave their rooms and come downstairs. 'Can Max come?' Craig asks his dad. 'No, you know he can't.'

'In your basket,' Stuart says to Max, as he trots through from the hall to the kitchen. 'Good-boy guard the house,' and he closes the front door.

The journey to Tricia's moms residential home is about 7 miles from where they live, and they arrive half an hour later. Stuart stops on the forecourt of the home, and no sooner has the vehicle become stationary than Craig is out like a shot. He rushes to the front door and rings the doorbell. The others get out and join him.

The door is opened by one of the carers called Christine. 'Hello,' she says, with a warm welcoming smile, as they all enter the hallway. 'Your Mom is in her room, I'll see if she is ready to receive you.' The family waits a few minutes until the carer returns. 'You can go up now she is ready to see you. Would you all like tea?' she asks. 'Yes please,' Tricia replies as they make their way upstairs led by Craig.

Having reached the landing he turns right, as he knows which is his nan's room and runs along the corridor to her. He pushes open the door and rushes in. His grandma is sitting in her chair by the window, with her feet on a pink dralon footstool. Despite her disability of walking she is a very healthy eighty-year-old and is the life and soul of the home. She occupies her time very well by keeping busy, ensuring she has numerous activities, and never seems to have a minute to herself.

Unable to contain his excitement he gives his nan a kiss. 'We're going on holiday on Saturday in a Plane.' 'Gosh that will be nice,' his nan replies, not quite understanding what has been told to her by Craig in his excitement.

The rest of the family enters the room and Claire gives her nan a kiss, and so do Tricia and Stuart. Tricia hands her mom the sweet- peas she has taken her. Her mom takes the flowers and thanks her for them. 'They're nice, have you got them from the garden?' she asks. 'Yes, shall I put them in some water for you?' 'Please, there's a vase under the sink.'

Tricia makes a search for the vase. 'What's this then, Craig says you are going on Holiday on Saturday?' nan asks Stuart. 'Yes, one of those last minute deals. We're going to Portugal.' 'Oh that will be nice,' nan replies. 'Can I go and play outside in the garden?' Craig asks his mother. 'Yes, but be quiet.'

A few minutes later there's a knock at the door. 'Come in,' Tricia's mother says, as the door opens and in walks the carer with a tray of tea. 'Thank you so much,' nan says as the carer places the tray of tea down and leaves the room.

'How are things Mom?' Tricia asks her mother. 'Oh Ok no problems. We had Communion yesterday, and I had my tea in the garden with Ester, and tomorrow I will be having my hair done.'

'How are things with you?' nan asks Claire. 'Oh, Ok Nan,' Claire says in a half-hearted way. 'What have you been up to?' her nan asks. 'Nothing much, been to town with Sarah. I have had a new Bikini and some Sandals for my Holiday.' 'Oh very nice,' her nan says. 'I suppose you will all be very busy now getting ready for your Holiday?' she adds. 'Yes,' Stuart replies. 'Pass me my Handbag,' nan asks, as Claire reaches for the bag on the bedside unit, and hands it to her. She opens it and takes a £10 note out, and gives it to Claire. 'Share this between you and Craig, buy yourselves some ice cream or something.' 'Oh thanks Nan, but you shouldn't.' Claire reaches over and gives her nan a kiss.

Stuart pours the tea for them all. Tricia places the sweet- peas in the bay window, sits on the bed and Stuart hands her a cup of tea. 'Our Katrina and Kate called this morning and stayed for coffee,' Tricia tells her mom. 'Oh yes she came to see me last week. She seemed a bit preoccupied.'

I know what Katrina was preoccupied with, Tricia thought to herself, 'Oh I suppose she is getting a bit stressed with her work, it's their busy time and she told me she was getting concerned about Kate's exam results.' Tricia replied. 'Kate told me she was expecting to do all right, so I don't know what Auntie Katrina is worried about.' Claire said.

Sobbing could be heard in the corridor outside, and nan's room door opens and in limps Craig crying his eyes out, followed by one of the carers. Tricia gets up from the bed and places her cup of tea on the tray. Craig approaches his mother for comfort. 'Now what have you done?' Tricia asks. 'I fell over,' he replied. 'I think he has hurt his leg,' the carer says. 'Roll up your trousers and let me have a look.' Craig won't let go of his mother, and he is still sobbing. 'Now come on let's roll up your trousers, I won't hurt you, but I need to see what you've done.' He reluctantly lets go of his mother and bends down and starts to roll his trouser legs up.

His mother sees he has grazed his knee on the left leg. 'Oh it's nothing too serious.' 'Do you want any First Aid equipment for it?' the carer asks. ' Yes please, just an Antiseptic Wipe will do.'

'Oh what a little Baby Waby we are then. Diddums bumped his little leggy weggy.' Claire says, in a very unsympathetic way.

Craig is not amused by his sister's sarcastic remarks at the pain and suffering he was going through. 'Shut up you,' he snaps back, and sticks his tongue out. 'Now now you two,' Tricia says, as she gets Craig to sit on the bed. 'You behave Claire, and stop winding your Brother up.'

The door opens, and the carer returns with an antiseptic wipe. 'Oh thanks,' Tricia says, as the carer hands her the wipe. She tears the packet open and unfolds the cloth. 'Now this might sting a little,' she says to Craig, as she starts to wipe the grazed area of skin. Craig cry's even more and falls back on the bed. 'Oh it isn't that bad you little baby,' Tricia says. 'It hurts,' he says. 'Diddums Diddums,' Claire says winding her brother up even more. 'I'll get you,' Craig says. 'Oh I am scared,' Claire remarks. 'Now I've told you Claire pack it in.'

Tricia finishes wiping the grazed skin. 'You'll be all right now. Up you get,' she says, and Craig starts to sit up and wipes the tears from his eyes.

'Do you want some Liquorice Allsorts?' his nan asks. 'Please,' he says. 'Go to the bottom draw and get the Bassett's tin out,' his nan says, and points towards her chest of drawers.

'Oh can I have one,' Claire asks, knowing full well her remark will cause a reaction from Craig. 'No, she's not having one,' Craig snaps back, as he reaches down and pulls open the chest of draws, and finds the Bassett tin just inside.

'Bring it here and I'll open it for you,' his nan says. Craig hands her the tin. 'Now which sort do you like best?' she asks. 'Do you like the ones with hundreds and thousands on, or the big yellow coconut ones?' she asks. 'Can I have that big yellow one?' he asks. 'Of course you can, but it'll cost you a big kiss.'

He takes the sweet and gives his nan a big kiss. 'What do you say?' Tricia asks. 'Thanks Nan.' 'Any one else like one?' as she offers the tin round to them all. 'Please,' Claire says. Craig is just about to react. 'Don't even think about it,' Tricia says, stopping Craig in his tracks.

The carer sees all is well now with Craig. 'Well he looks Ok now,' the carer says, 'I'll leave you to it.' 'Thanks,' Tricia says, as the carer leaves the room.

Tricia looks at her watch. 'Good God look at the time. We'll have to go,' she says, 'Now you'll be all right while we're gone?' 'Yes, now have a good holiday and send us a card,' her mom replies. 'We will.' Tricia reaches down and gives her mom a kiss. They all in turn give her a kiss as they leave. 'I'll wave from the window,' she says.

Nan makes her way to the window, and looks down as Stuart's Range Rover drives slowly down the drive towards the road, as they all wave good-bye and drive off.

Chapter 10

Having had a very busy and tiring day, both Stuart and Tricia have an early night. Stuart tosses, and turns, and finally he manages to lie on his right side facing the window, and starts to try and get some sleep.

Tricia has her bedside table light on and is reading her book. Suddenly she puts her book down and gives Stuart a dig in his back with her elbow. 'Are you awake?' she asks. 'No, I wasn't, but I am now,' Stuart remarks, 'I was trying to get some sleep,' he says.

'Oh you couldn't have been asleep, you have only just turned the light out.' 'What do you want?' Stuart asks.

'I was just thinking, do you remember the holiday we had in Cornwall staying in a Villa, when we had a plague of Fly's, and you spent an hour and a half killing them before I would let you get to Bed?' 'Yes,' he says, 'Our Craig was only a month old at the time.' 'Yes, so why are you talking about it now, at this time of night. Get on with your book, and let me have some sleep?'

Stuart thumps the pillow with his fist, and then closes his eyes, but Tricia won't stop. 'Well I hope we don't have them in Portugal, because if we do, I am on the first plane back home. They were awful. Do you remember, they came up out of the floorboards in the bedroom, and from the gaps in the wall, they were everywhere. God they make me crawl just thinking about them?'

'Well stop thinking about it, and let me get to sleep.' 'The man next door but two was also plagued with them, and a family a few doors down. I wonder where the flies came from?' she says, but there was now no reply from Stuart.

She gives him another dig in the back. 'Are you listening to me?' she says. 'God you can be a pain sometimes,' Stuart snaps. 'Well I am just warning you if there are any Flies out there in Portugal I am off.' 'Good, I might get some sleep then,' Stuart says, as he thumps his pillow again and settles back down.

Tricia picks her book up, and carries on reading, until eventually tiredness overcomes her and she also falls asleep.

Stuart eventually wakes up, and realises it is morning, and he turns over to find Tricia is not there, but he hears the shower working and assumes she's having her morning shower. The bedroom door swings open and in strolls Max and he wonders round to Stuart, and puts his front paws up on the bed and gives him a lick on his face.

'Hello fella,' Stuart reaches out and rubs Max's head. 'I suppose you want to go up the garden, well you will just have to wait a minute Mom is in the shower.'

Max is not impressed, so he jumps up on the bed right on top of Stuart. Stuart is now getting the message. 'Ok, Ok, get off, I am getting up.' Max jumps down and Stuart gets out of bed and goes downstairs to let Max out.

He puts the kettle on, and gets the teapot out and a mug, and starts to make a cup of tea for himself.

While he waits for the kettle to boil he looks up the garden. Got to get the lawns mowed today and the garden tidied up, he thinks to himself. If I have time, I must wash the car and check it over for oil and water.

The kettle boils and switches itself off; he makes the tea and lets it stand for a while. He walks over to the wall cupboard and gets a biscuit out of the tin. He then pours his tea into the mug and gives it a stir.

Although he is still in his pyjamas, he wonders outside, and sits on the garden bench under the kitchen window to drink his tea, and looks at the various plants in the garden that will require his special attention.

His thoughts wonder round the tasks, such as the cosmos will require the dead heads removed, and the roses as well. I'll have to water and feed the tubs, and the hanging baskets, no doubt there will be other things.

He continues to take the morning air, and finishes his tea in a slow and meaningful way, enjoying the early morning peace and quiet. The sun is shining, and he points his face towards it and feels the warming suns rays on his face. God this is bliss he thinks to himself, as he wallows in the occasion.

With all the household now fully awake, and breakfast over, Tricia finds she has yet more washing to contend with, but this is the last and final wash which she hopes will be dry in the heat of the day by lunch time.

Stuart has the lawn mower well in action when the doorbell rings. 'I'll get it,' Craig shouts as he opens the door to find Simon standing there holding his bike. 'Are you coming over the school field to play footie?' he asks. 'Yes, but I'll just ask Mom if its Ok.' 'Mom, can I go and play over the school field with Simon?' 'Yes, but mind what you're doing over there, and stay near the road end.' 'Ok.' Craig leaves the house and gets his bike out of the garage. He joins Simon and they ride off to the school field situated at the rear of their house.

'What do you want me to do for you to-day Mom?' Claire asks.

'You can make a start on your packing if you like. If you start off by putting all your underwear in first and your shoes. Put some of your pants and socks inside your shoes, that'll make some more room for other things. Wrap your shoes inside some old carrier bags to keep the clothes clean. Then put your trousers and skirts in, and finally your tops. Try and fold them neatly and as flat as possible. If anything needs ironing do them. Don't forget everything you want to take with you must be in your case. You can have only one handbag with you, and no sharp objects in it like scissors, and make it as light as possible. Put all your toilet things inside your toilet bag, and that'll have to go in your case as well.' Tricia says. 'What about the weight of the case?' Claire asks. 'It mustn't be more than 20 kilogram's, but you should be well under that, it's us who will have to watch the weight,' Tricia remarks.

'Ok,' Claire says, and she makes her way upstairs to start on her packing.

Stuart has finished mowing the back lawn, and he wonders into the garage and gets his lawn edger down, and starts trimming the lawn edges.

It's a tedious task, which does however require a certain amount of concentration, but not all the time, and his mind wanders onto different things while he walks round the garden.

I hope the plane isn't late taking off, it's a pain hanging around the departure lounge and the kids get restless, but as we're on an early flight things might be on time he thinks to himself. I mustn't forget to take some film for the camera, and I think I'll travel in my lightweight checked trousers and suede shoes. I am not taking any rainwear. If it rains we'll have to buy something out there.

Having finished cutting the lawn edges, he replaces the edge trimmer and puts his kneepads on. He gets the dustbin lid, and kneels down, and starts to gather the bits of grass cuttings from the garden, trimming the dead heads off the cosmos and roses as he goes round. Although some people think gardening is a chore, he finds it very therapeutic. It's warm work in this heat, but it must be done.

Tricia wonders out into the garden to Stuart and hands him a glass of lemon squash. 'Oh thanks. I need that,' he says, as he takes the glass from her and has a long drink. 'How's it going?' she asks. 'Ok nearly finished the back,' he replies.

'I think the plants could do with a water?' she says. 'Yes I'll do them to-night,' he adds. 'Those Cosmos are lovely, we must get some more next year,' she says, as she looks at the pink daisy like flowers in abundance.

Tricia goes back into the house, and brings the washing out, and commences to peg it on the rotary clothesline.

Stuart carries on with his gardening, his mind drifts away from what he's doing. I think I would like a summerhouse built up here at the top of the garden. He recalls having seen some at a local garden centre, which really impressed him at the time. He looks at the space available, and wonders if one could be fitted in the area. He starts to pace it out. It appears to be about five yards by five yards. That would be fifteen foot by fifteen foot, and it faces south. If I altered the lawn and flowerbeds here and there, levelled off the south side, and slabbed the north side, I could get it in here by the garage.

'Tricia, come over here a minute will you?' Stuart asks. 'Yes when I have finished pegging these clothes out.'

He carries on studying the space in the garden, which is currently lawned. He walks back towards the house and picks up two garden chairs, and carries them back to the top of the garden, and puts them down on the grass side by side, and sits on one, imagining he was inside the new summerhouse as Tricia walks across the garden towards him.

'You haven't got time to sit there admiring your handy work,' Tricia says. 'Shut up, and sit down, there's something I want to discuss with you,' Stuart says. 'That sounds ominous,' Tricia replies.

'What do you think about the idea of having a Summerhouse built here?' he asks her. 'What's brought that idea on?' 'Well I was thinking, wouldn't it be nice to come up here and just relax, and chill out with a gin and tonic on a summers evening.' 'Yes I suppose it would, but how much is it going to cost?' 'I don't know exactly, but I suppose I can cost it out, but what do you think of the idea?' 'Yes I think it would be rather nice, it would smarten the garden, and I suppose we could do it in stages to spread the cost out a bit, but I would need to see some houses first.' 'Yes I know, and when we get back off holiday we can have a look one Sunday afternoon, there might even be a sale on, you never know.' 'I hope you are not thinking of doing all the work yourself?' 'No, I would ask Steve if he would give me a hand with the basics, like slabbing and levelling the garden, but I could manage the rest easy enough.'

An agreement about the issue was now settled between them, and Tricia went back into the house, and Stuart carried on with the gardening, feeling chuffed with himself about the prospects of having a summerhouse.

Chapter 11

Craig and Simon have reached the school field, and find Mark and Andrew fellow classmates are also playing football. 'Do you want to make a team up and play with us?' Mark asks Craig. 'If you like,' he says, as the two boys lean their bikes against the hedge.

The four boys start to play football kicking and passing the ball between themselves, and generally having fun, when a gang of older boys come towards them from the back of the school field. The gang walk towards the boys, and one of them runs and kicks the ball from Simon to his mates. The four boys feel threatened by the gang's presence, Craig bravely says, 'Give us our ball back.' 'Come and get it Punk,' one of the older boys says, as they pass the ball between themselves. 'It's not yours, give it back,' Craig demands in a brave voice.

'What are you going to do about it Tich?' One of the older boys says, who is dressed in baggy jeans with a sweatshirt on, and a baseball cap on his head turned backwards. 'I'll get my Dad,' Craig says. 'Oh I am scared,' he remarks as his mates laugh and kick the ball towards him.

'Now listen Kid, if you know what's good for you, I would keep your trap shut, or I'll shut it for you,' the boy says, as he leans down towards Craig threatening him with his clenched fist.

'I am not scared of you,' Craig says. 'Well you should be Kid,' as the boy grabs Craig by his shirt and lifts him off the ground, and brings him up face to face, and stares him in the eyes. 'I'll give you a good smack in the mouth. Now piss off,' he says. He drops Craig on the grass, and the boy walks towards his mates and they continue to pass the ball to each other.

One of the other members of the gang kicks the ball so hard and so high up in the air, it lands in the tree and stays there.

'Get that Punk,' the boy said, as his mates start laughing. 'Come on let's leave it to 'em to get it down,' and they all walk off the field towards town.

'Are you alright?' Simon says, as he kneels down by Craig. 'Yes, they didn't scare me,' he says. 'Well they scared me,' Simon says. 'What are we going to do about the Ball?' Mark asks. 'I'll go and get it. Give us a shin up,' Craig says.

The lads run over to the tree, and help Craig to get up. He manages to get hold of a branch with his hands and swings his legs round it. He then climbs onto the next branch and gives it a shake, and the ball falls to the ground. However Craig loses his balance, and his foot slips off the branch he is standing on, and he is swinging by his hands.

'Look out', Simon shouts, 'the branch is going to break'. A loud crack is heard. Craig hangs on and tries to get a foot on another branch, but it's too far away. Crack, snap, the branch isn't strong enough to hold him and it breaks, and he falls to the ground with a thud, as he lands on his back, and then silence.

He is motionless as Simon rushes over to him and kneels down by his side. 'Are you alright?' he asks, but there is no response from Craig. Mark says, 'He's dead.' Andrew says, 'No he's not, I can see he is still breathing.' 'What are we going to do?' Andrew says. 'I think we should tell his Mom?' says Mark. 'Yes Ok, I'll go and get her. You two stay here,' Simon says, as he gets on his bike and rides for all his worth round to Craig's house.

Craig's dad is mowing the front lawn, as Simon rushes up, gasping for breath, 'Mr Osborn, Craig's fallen out of a tree, and he won't wake up,' Simon says, having ridden so hard to tell Craig's family what has happened. 'Where is he?' Stuart asks. 'He's over the school field,' Simon says. Stuart leaves the mowing and runs in to tell Tricia. 'Phone for an Ambulance will you, Craig's fallen out of a Tree, and he's over the school field.' 'Oh my God,' Tricia says in a state of panic.

Stuart runs down the drive led by Simon on his bike, as they make their way towards the school field. He reaches the field, and sees Craig lying there at the foot of a tree. 'What happened?' Stuart asks Mark and Andrew.

'Some boys kicked our ball up the tree and Craig went to get it, but the branch broke, and he fell down, and now he won't wake up,' Mark said.

Stuart kneels down by Craig, and taps his face trying to bring him round. 'Craig wake up,' Stuart says, 'Come on wake up,' Stuart repeats himself, but there is no response. Being a Teacher, Stuart is aware of first aid, and he checks to see if Craig is breathing. He looks at his chest, and sees it rising and falling in a gentle manner.

He must be knocked out Stuart thinks to himself, as he hears the distant sound of a wailing siren, which seems to be getting closer, then the tone changes into a two tone sound. Stuart looks towards the road and sees Tricia and Claire running towards them across the field.

'He's knocked out,' Stuart shouts to Tricia, as she gets closer. 'He'll be alright in a bit,' Stuart says trying to reassure her, as Tricia reaches them.

They all see the ambulance stop in the road near to where they are. One of the attendants makes his way across the field towards them, while the other opens the back door of the ambulance and steps inside, and removes a canvas stretcher and makes his way towards them.

Stuart says to the ambulanceman as he reaches him, 'He's fallen out of the tree and I think he's knocked himself out.' 'Ok lets have a look at him.' The ambulanceman kneels down beside Craig and removes a small torch from his shirt pocket, and opens Craig's eyelids, and shines the torch into his eyes, but there is no response. 'What's the lads name?' the ambulanceman asks. 'Its Craig, I am his Father,' Stuart said. 'I am going to put a neck brace on him just in case he has hurt himself.'

The ambulanceman removes a plastic neck brace from his medical kit, and gently lifts Craig's head up, and slides the brace under his head and fastens it, securing it in a ridged state.

The two ambulancemen slide a ridged board under Craig and gently lift him onto the stretcher. 'We will have to take him to Hospital, are you coming with us?' the ambulanceman enquires. 'No, my Wife and Daughter will, if that's ok,' Stuart said. 'Yes of course.' 'Which Hospital are you taking him to?' 'The Queens,' the ambulanceman replies. 'I'll see you there,' Stuart says to Tricia.

The three boys watch, as Craig is stretchered off the field into the waiting ambulance. 'Do you think they will put the siren on?' Simon asks. 'Yeah, and I bet it goes ever so fast,' Andrew remarked as they watch Craig being placed into the ambulance, and Tricia and Claire sit with him in the back as the ambulance starts to make its way to the hospital.

Tricia is quite worried that Craig still hasn't woken up. The ambulance driver calls his base on the radio. 'One young male to the Queens unconscious. Mother in attendance.' 'Received Bravo 4,' the operator replies.

'Don't worry Misses, he'll be alright,' the ambulanceman says to Tricia.

'Trust our Craig to make a drama out of it.' Claire says to her mother.
'Now don't start Claire, I can't be doing with that right now,' Tricia says, as the ambulance gathers speed and the two tones sound.

The ambulance approaches some traffic lights near to where they live, which are on red. The driver slows down, but with his two-tone horns blearing away, and his blue lights flashing, the opposing traffic give way to him. He waves his hand to thank them, as he accelerates on towards the hospital.

Suddenly Craig's head moves slightly, and his eyes flicker, and eventually open. 'Ok Son how are you? You've been knocked out, but you'll be Ok, your Mom is here,' the ambulanceman says to Craig.

Tricia leans over towards Craig and squeezes his hand. 'How are you?' she says. 'My head hurts,' 'Try not to move Son, you're wearing a neck brace, and I want to keep it on until we reach the Hospital,' the ambulanceman says.

'Hello trouble,' Claire says in an unsympathetic catty manner, but really it's a front to keep up the tough sister and brother rapour they have between themselves. Never the less she was quite worried, but she didn't want to show it to Craig.

Craig is not impressed by her remarks, and offers no reply, but manages to look across at her with a cold stare.

The ambulance starts to slow down, and the two-tone siren is switched off as they arrive at the emergency department at the Queens hospital, the ambulance stops at the main entrance. The back doors open, the two-ambulancemen start to remove the stretcher, and wheel Craig into the hospital.

They barge through the clear plastic doors, and enter a short corridor leading to the examination area of the A & E department of the hospital.

'Would you go to the Casualty Desk and book Craig in?' one of the ambulancemen says to Tricia, 'It's through those doors. (He points to the right) We'll take him into the unit and your Daughter can come with us,' he adds.

Craig is wheeled into a cubicle, and lifted onto the bed by the ambulancemen. 'Now don't worry Son, you'll be alright, a Nurse will see you in a minute.' They start to move the stretcher away as a nurse approaches. 'Thanks,' Claire says to the ambulancemen. 'Your Mom I'll be here in a minute,' the ambulanceman replies.

'Now young man what have you been up to?' the nurse enquires. She is a West Indian, and a very buxom lady, but with a very big warm welcoming smile.

'I went up this tree to get our ball back, which some big kids had kicked up, and I fell down, and then it all went blank. I remember seeing a bright light, and I heard music playing, and a grey haired old man conducting the Orchestra waving me away, and then I woke up in the Ambulance,' Craig said. 'Well I never,' the nurse replied.

Tricia finds them all in the casualty unit, as the nurse shines a little torch into Craig's eyes, and the pupils dilate, which is a good sign.

'How is he Nurse, I am his Mother?' 'Oh he's fine, but we'll have to X Ray him, and possibly keep him in overnight for observations, because of the bang to his head, but don't you worry love, we'll look after him good and proper won't we,' the nurse replies, and gives a big smile to Craig.

The nurse draws the curtains round the bed. 'A Doctor will be along shortly to see you,' she says as she leaves. Tricia sits on the edge of the bed and holds Craig's hand.

The area around the bed has a chair and a cabinet with various metal dishes, and paper bowls which look like hats, but Tricia realises these are for when people are sick. She sees oxygen masks and pipes over the bed, and a blood pressure machine on top of the cabinet, and that hospital smell, which lingers in your nose for weeks.

Seeing these items gives her concern, and awakens her stressful feelings of the situation she has suddenly found herself in. Will her only son be all right, she thinks to herself, as she looks at Craig's face, as he lies there with his head locked into a neck brace.

Trying not to show her true inner feelings, she squeezes his hand. 'It won't be long now the Doctor will soon be here,' she says to Craig. She turns to Claire, 'I wonder how much longer your Dad's going to be?' 'Do you want me to go and see if I can find him?' Claire asks. 'Would you?' 'I won't be long,' and Claire swishes the curtain back and leaves the cubicle.

Tricia stands up, and leans over Craig so she can see his face, and he can see hers. 'So how did this all happen then. What were you doing up the tree in the first place?'

Before he could make any reply, the cubicle curtains are opened, and in steps a doctor in a white coat, with the cheery West Indian nurse behind him.

'Hello, I am Doctor Mckinner.' Doctor Mckinner was aged about forty, and Tricia found him very attractive, as she looked up at him, and saw his very sexy paper thin gold glasses perched on his nose, with his dark black hair, and slightly greying temples. He was about six feet tall, nice and slim, and wearing a plaid tie, which seemed to go with his Scottish accent, adding to his colourful appearance. Wow, Tricia thought, he can examine me anytime.

'Now what has this young man been up to?' 'I fell out of a tree,' Craig replies. 'Well, that's not the best thing in the world to do is it,' the doctor remarks. 'These big kids kicked our ball up the tree, and I went to get it, when the branch broke, and I fell.' 'Well we will have to see what we can do to get you playing again as quickly as possible.' 'We're going on holiday on Saturday on a plane to Algarve,' Craig tells the doctor in an excited manner, and for once he managed to say the correct pronunciation of Algarve. 'Well that's nice, so we had better make sure you are fit to fly then,' the doctor replies.

'Now, I am just going to shine a bright light into your eyes.' The doctor removes his pen torch from his coat pocket, and shines it into Craig's eyes. Can you now move your arms for me'? Craig lifts his arms up and down, 'Can you bend them?' Craig bends his arms. 'Is there any pain?' 'No.' 'Now can you do the same with your legs?' Craig bends his legs. 'Can you feel any pain?' 'No.'

'Good. I think we should have an X-Ray taken on the skull, and I think he should be kept in overnight in the Children's Ward for observations. Would you make the arrangements Nurse?' 'Yes,' she says. 'I'll probably see you in the morning young man. Let me know when the X-Rays have been taken so I can see the results.' 'Yes Doctor,' the nurse replies. The doctor leaves the cubicle.

'I'll arrange for a Porter to take you up to the X-Ray department, so just wait with him will you,' the nurse says as she leaves the cubicle.

Tricia turns to Craig. 'So, you're going to have an X-Ray, its nothing to worry about, they are just going to take some special pictures of your head to make sure you haven't fractured your skull.' 'I want a wee,' Craig replies. 'Oh God, you don't do you?' 'Yes.' 'You would wouldn't you. Well just see if you can hold it?' 'I can't.' 'Well you will have to.'

'I can't, I really want a wee Mam Now.' Tricia gets up and opens the cubicle curtains, and sees the nurse the other side of the room filling in some forms, so she walks over to her. 'Sorry to bother you, but Craig wants the toilet. He wants a wee.' 'Oh not to worry my love give him this.' She reaches under the work area where she is standing and hands Tricia a grey cardboard bottle. 'He can use this.' 'Oh thanks.' Tricia walks back to the cubicle.

'Here you'll have to use this.' She helps him, and between them they manage to use the bottle, just as Stuart and Claire return.

'How are things?' Stuart asks. 'A Doctor's examined him and he has got to have an X-Ray on his head.' Claire stops Tricia in mid sentence. 'They won't find anything in there.' 'Now stop it Claire,' Tricia remarks. 'Shurrup you,' Craig replies. 'Now you two stop it, and he is going to have to stay in overnight for observations. The Doctor has examined his arms and legs, and they seem ok.' 'Good,' Stuart replies.

'We're just waiting for a Porter to take him to X-Ray, and that's about it. Oh he has just had a wee.' 'Well that's good,' Stuart remarks. 'Have you had a drink or anything?' Tricia asks Stuart. 'No, but why don't you and Claire go to the waiting room there's a tea machine there, I passed it on the way in.'

Claire guides her mom in the direction of the waiting room. They find the tea machine, and Tricia puts in some coins, and presses the keypad marked 'Tea no sugar'. The cup drops down, and hot water runs into it, and eventually stops.

She picks it up. It's too hot to take any quantity, but she does manage a very small sip. Claire puts in 50p, and manages to get a can of coke from the machine. They both find a seat among the many people in the waiting room. Tricia looks outside and sees the sun is still shining. She takes another sip of tea and ponders on the events, which are taking place, and hopes the outcome is good.

Chapter 12

A porter has arrived at last to take Craig up to x-ray and he wheels Craig in his bed accompanied by the nurse, and followed by Stuart to the x-ray department.

Tricia and Claire finish their drinks 'Well I suppose we had better get back and see what's happening,' Tricia says to Claire.

They reach the Emergency Unit only to find the cubicle is empty. 'They must have gone to the X-Ray department,' Tricia says. 'We had better join them?'

They wander along the corridors following the signposts until they reach the x-ray department. 'Ah, here you are, hiding from me,' Tricia says to Craig, as she sees them both in the waiting area. Craig was still lying flat on his bed. 'They have done the X-Rays, (Stuart points to the large brown envelope lying on Craig's legs) we are just waiting for the Porter to take us back to A & E,' Stuart says. 'You haven't been long.' 'No, we came just right, and went in more or less straight away,' Stuart tells Tricia.

'What was it like?' Tricia asks Craig. 'Ok, they put me on this bed, and then this thing came over my head, and I had to keep very still,' Craig replied.

With that, a very stout man in his late fifties approaches them in a grey porters jacket. 'Craig Osborn,' he says. 'Yes that's us,' Stuart replies.

'Right it's back to A & E then young man.' The porter releases the brake holding the wheel on the bed, and he starts to push Craig's bed from behind his head, and feet forward. The family follow them to A & E. The porter carefully manoeuvres the bed back into the cubicle area and puts the brake back on. He reaches for the x-ray pictures and starts to draw the curtains. 'The Nurse will be with you in a minute.' 'Thanks,' Stuart replies.

The porter hands the x-rays over to the West Indian nurse and she puts them on her desk. 'Thanks,' she says to the porter. 'Could you take the lady in 5 to the plaster room she is in a wheelchair?' 'Yes, no problems,' he replies. The nurse picks up the telephone and pages Dr Mckinner.

'I suppose we will have to wait a while for the Doctor to come, so I am off for a cup of Tea if no one minds,' Stuart says. 'Yes ok, but don't be too long,' Tricia remarks.

Half an hour goes by, and Stuart still hasn't come back, nor has the doctor. 'Go and find your Dad,' Tricia says to Claire. Claire leaves the cubicle, but as she does she puts her head back through the curtains.

'The Doctor is looking at the X-Rays with the Nurse,' she says in a soft tone to her mother. 'Oh good, so be quick, and get your Dad,' Tricia says.

Claire walks as fast as she can towards the waiting room, but meets her dad on the way. 'Mom wants you back, the Doctor is looking at the X-Rays now.' 'Oh good,' Stuart replies.

The curtain opens and Dr Mckinner and the nurse enter the cubicle.
'Mrs Osborn I have the results of the X-Rays,' Dr Mckinner says to Tricia, and at the same time Stuart and Claire follow the doctor into the cubicle, much to the relief of Tricia. 'Oh hello Doctor,' Stuart says. 'I was just saying I have the results of the X-Rays, and there are no fractures of the skull or neck. It looks as if you have a tough young man here Mrs Osborn. However, I would like to keep him in overnight just to be on the safe side. We will admit you into the Children's Ward. Nurse James here will fill you in on the details, and you can stay with him if you wish, and I'll see you in the morning.' 'Thank you Doctor,' Tricia says, as Doctor Mckinner leaves.

'You're a very lucky chap,' nurse James says to Craig. 'I always thought he had a thick skull,' Claire remarks. 'Shurrup you,' Craig replies.

'Now you two, I have told you Claire. Sorry about that, its Brother and Sister love,' Tricia says, as she glares scornfully at Claire. 'I know what you mean, I have two kids myself, and they are always going at each other,' nurse James replies. 'Now what we have to do is to take this neck brace off and get you comfortable.'

Nurse James then starts to remove the neck brace. Having removed it she says, 'How's that, is that more comfortable?' 'Yes,' says Craig. 'You can sit up now, but do it slowly you may feel a little light headed.'

Craig raises himself up, as Tricia reaches under his shoulders to assist him.

'How's that feel?' nurse James asks. 'Ok,' Craig replies. Nurse James readjusts the bed and puts a pillow behind him, and then removes the hardboard he has been lying on. 'Now I bet you could do with a drink of juice couldn't you?' Nurse James asks Craig. 'Please,' he replies. 'Right I will see what I can find you.' She leaves the cubicle area.

'So what are we going to do as he has to stay in overnight?' Tricia asks Stuart. He looks at his watch. 'Its half past three. Why don't you and Claire find the canteen and have something to eat. I'll stay with Craig, and when you have finished come back here and I can go. By then I should think they'll be ready to transfer him to the Children's Ward.'

'What about all the packing for the holiday, and all the things we have to do tomorrow?' 'Don't worry; it'll get sorted tomorrow. Now here's a tenner, off you go.' Stuart reaches into his wallet and hands Tricia a ten-pound note. 'Well I hope you are right,' Tricia remarks, in a concerned and worried manner. 'I've said it will be ok, didn't I,' Stuart replies sternfully.

Tricia and Claire leave the emergency ward and make their way to the canteen, but Tricia is still worried, and no matter how reassuring Stuart is, her concerns will not go away.

The curtain is drawn back around the bed as nurse James returns with a glass of ice-cold orange juice for Craig. 'Now, just you try this and see if you don't feel better.' She hands Craig the drink, and within seconds he has drunk the glass full. 'My goodness, I think you were ready for that' she says. 'Could I have another one?' Craig asks. 'Excuse me young man, what else do we say?' Stuart asks checking his manners. 'Sorry, please.' 'That's better,' Stuart remarks. 'Yes I think I had better bring the jug don't you?' Nurse James smiles as she walks off to get the jug of orange juice.

The ward telephone is heard to ring, and she picks up the receiver 'Hello, Nurse James speaking.' The voice on the telephone passes on a message and she replaces the receiver. She then returns to Craig with the jug of juice. 'There, now let's see if we can quench that thirst of yours,' and she pours Craig another glass. 'That was the Children's Ward they are ready for you now, and they will send a porter in about half an hour to take you there.' 'Thanks,' Stuart remarks.

As Stuart sits by Craig's bed, he begins to think of all the jobs he has to fit into today, when Tricia comes back. I think I had better get off back home for a while and get things moving, and return later with some night-clothes for Craig and something for Tricia, as it seems she will have to stay the night. God I could do without this. It couldn't have happened at a worse time.

Don't panic. That's a fine remark he thinks to himself at a time like this. Don't panic.

The happy smiling porter interrupts Stuart's thoughts. 'Craig Osborn?' the porter asks. 'That's us.' Stuart replies. 'Well we're off to the Children's Ward,' the porter then starts to move the bed. Nurse James hands the porter Craig's notes. 'Good luck Craig. You will enjoy it up there.' 'Thanks for everything,' Stuart replies. 'Tell Tricia where we've gone.' 'Yes no problems, bye.' Craig is then wheeled swiftly along the corridor to the lift.

The children's ward is a totally different environment from the emergency ward. Craig sees brightly coloured pictures on the walls, and toys seem to be everywhere. He also sees other moms and dads, and older children and younger ones, and even young babies in cots. He sees a boy with his leg in plaster, and suspended in the air on pulleys. He then suddenly finds his bed is parked opposite this boy, next to an older girl who has her mother with her, but he can't see what's the matter with the girl, as she seems to be asleep.

The mother smiles and says hello to Craig and Stuart, as the porter parks the bed. 'The Nurse will be with you in a minute,' the porter says, as he walks off and hands the notes into the nurse's station.

The mother of the girl in the next bed to Craig is very pretty and petite, with blonde hair. She looks up at Stuart and says, 'It's lovely in here, the nurses are really kind and thoughtful. What's the matter with your boy?' she asks. 'It's Craig and I am his Dad Stuart. He fell out of a Tree and was knocked out. He's in here for observations overnight. What's the matter with your Daughter?' he asks. 'She has just had her Appendics out, and they have just brought her back from Theatre, so she's a bit sleepy at the moment.' 'His Mother and Sister will be here in a minute, they have just gone to the Canteen for something to eat,' Stuart says.

'God, I could do with a drink and something to eat as well, but I don't like to leave her. Her Dad is abroad on business, and isn't due back until Saturday, and he doesn't know anything about this.' 'Well I'll keep an eye on her, why don't you slip off and if she wakes up I'll tell one of the Nurses.' 'Are you sure?' 'Yes of course. Now go on and have that break, it sounds like you need one.' 'Thanks ever so much, I won't be long.' 'What's her name by the way?' Stuart asks. 'Angela,' the mother replies as she leaves the ward.

Sitting there quietly, Stuart starts to think to himself when he was Craig's age having his tonsils out. The trauma of it has faded over the years, but the event is still in his thoughts even now. Remembering only bits and pieces. He remembered going to his doctor with his mother and having a wooden stick put in his throat, and the doctor saying, 'I think they will have to come out.' He also remembered being in a room with lots of other children all in white gowns, and a vague memory of sitting in the hospital bed, and spitting blood, and a nurse giving him ice cream. That was a good memory, especially the ice cream, which was pink and white, and really soothed his throat.

He remembered his mother collecting him from the hospital and having a small gift for being such a brave little soldier, but what was that gift. His memory was straining hard to recall it, but it wouldn't come as he stared hard into space trying to remember.

'Ah there you are. Are you all right?' the voice said, as Stuart looked up with a blank expression on his face. 'Oh hello, sorry I was miles away,' as he saw Tricia and Claire standing there, having made it to the ward from the canteen.

'Is everything alright?' Tricia asks. 'Yes we have just arrived, and we are waiting for the Nurse to see us.'

A very slim young looking nurse wearing black trousers, and a white tunic jacket, and short black hair, quickly approaches them. 'I am Liz; sorry for keeping you waiting, just one of those little crisis's which happen now and again. Now it's Craig isn't it?' Craig nods his head. 'How are you feeling?' she asks, in a light-hearted manner with a big broad smile. 'Ok,' he replies. 'Now I understand you fell out of a Tree, is that right?' Craig nods his head again. 'Well I think what we should do with you is let you have some rest, and if you like you can stay here to night with your Mom or Dad. Would you like that?' He nods his head yet again.

The nurse then speaks to Tricia and Stuart. 'Everything looks ok with the X Rays and tests, and there seems nothing to worry about, but when children have had a bang to their heads we like to keep an eye on them for a while, just to make sure nothing untoward happens, its just routine. Are you happy with that?' Both Tricia and Stuart reply, 'Yes that's ok with us.'

'Would one of you wish to stay with him tonight?' Liz asks. 'Craig do you want me or your Dad to stay with you tonight?' Tricia asks. 'No, I am ok. I'll be all right.' 'Are you sure?' 'Yes,' he replies.

'Well if that's all right with you Nurse?' Tricia asks. ' Yes that's fine by me, and should anything happen we have your Telephone Number so we can give you a ring.'

Tricia walks towards Craig and gives him a big kiss. 'You'll be Ok, your Dad and I will collect you in the morning. Now be a good boy, and behave yourself, and don't give the Nurse any trouble, do you hear?'

'Oh stop fussing!' he replies.

'Don't Pick your Nose either,' Claire says.

'Bog off you,' Craig scornfully replies to his sister, and puts his tongue out to her as well.

'Now you two stop it,' Tricia says. 'The bang to his head hasn't effected his sense of humour,' Claire remarks sarcastically.

'Brother and Sisterly love,' Tricia says as she looks at Liz, feeling embarrassed by the children's remarks to each other. 'Can I have a word,' Tricia asks Liz as she moves away from Craig's bed. 'We're going on holiday on Saturday to the Algarve.' 'Oh nice,' Liz says. 'Well I was wondering, is he going to be all right to fly?' 'Well if he has a good nights sleep, and he has no other symptoms, he should be ok, but we will have to see how he is in the morning, but don't worry I am sure he will be fine.'

'Right, come on you lot, let's go,' Tricia says to Stuart and Claire. 'We have some things to do back home. Bye darling, sleep well, and we'll see you in the morning.'

Just as they are leaving, Angela's mom meets them at the ward door. 'We're just going, but she hasn't woken up yet and the Nurse is with her now,' Stuart says. 'Oh right thanks, bye.' The family moves along the corridor on their way out. 'Who was that?' Tricia asks. 'That was the Mother of the girl in the next bed. She has just been to the canteen for something to eat, and I was just keeping an eye on her Daughter if she woke up from the Anaesthetic.' 'Oh that was good of you,' Tricia remarks.

Having arrived back home and parked the Range Rover, they enter the house. Max is there to greet them, and he's pleased to see them back, but he's looking to see where Craig is. Yet despite the fact they can't talk they do have an uncanny way of being aware of things that are not quite right. 'Craig's in hospital,' Stuart says to Max, as he bends down and gives him some fuss, expecting the dog to understand what has been said to him. 'Well I had better get some tea on,' Tricia says. 'And I think I had better finish off the front lawn,' Stuart replies, as Claire dashes upstairs. She enters her bedroom and phones Sarah to tell her about the events of the day.

Stuart starts to finish off the lawn. 'Is everything all right?' He looks round to his right and sees Sandra from next door on her driveway.

'Oh hello,' Stuart says, as he leaves his lawn mower and walks across his drive to talk to her. 'It's our Craig, he fell out of one of the tree's over by the School and was knocked out. We have had to take him to Hospital. He's Ok now they are just keeping him in overnight for observations.' ' Oh my God. Well I thought something was up as you all dashed off so fast. How's Tricia?' 'She's Ok, go and see her if you like the back gates open.' 'Right,' and with that, Sandra makes her way to the back gate to talk with Tricia.

'I know he can be a little sod sometimes, but I must admit I was quite worried seeing him lying there out cold. Dad was brilliant and kept his cool. I went with Mom in the Ambulance, and then he woke up on the way to the Hospital.' Claire is talking on her mobile phone to Sarah, and filling her in on the details of the events. 'We left him in the Children's Ward. Mom told him to behave himself and I said in a loud voice so the nurse could hear, 'Don't pick your nose,' they both burst out laughing. 'You are rotten,' Sarah says. 'It didn't half make him blush I tell you. I spotted one or two very nice young male nurses around. I felt like saying, 'Oh I feel faint nurse,' and seeing if one of them would come and save me.' They both laugh. 'It would have been just my luck for some old biddy to have saved me.' ' You're crackers do you know that,' Sarah says. 'I know, but it would have been a laugh.' They both start giggling.

'Are you still going on holiday?' Sarah asks. 'You bet I am, even if it is without Craig. You'd look after him wouldn't you?' 'You have to be joking,' Sarah replies. 'You would, you're my best mate.' ' Get knotted,' Sarah replies. 'I am only kidding,' Claire remarks.

Chapter 13

It was late when the family went to bed Thursday night due to the confusion of the day, which put them behind with their plans.

However there was still time to catch up on the packing, but it was going to be a busy Friday, as they still had to get Craig from the hospital, and take the animals to the kennels, as well as everything else.

Tricia was up earlier than the rest of the family and combing her hair in the dining room mirror, as Stuart enters the kitchen still in his pyjamas.

'Morning love,' he says, as he stretches his arms in the air. 'God I'm knackered,' as he looks at Tricia in the dining room combing her hair. 'You've missed a bit,' he says. Tricia carries on combing her hair, but looks at him through the mirror, and puts her tongue out at him.

He reaches for the kettle, and puts some water in it, and switches it on 'Do you want a cuppa?' he asks. 'No I've had one,' she replies. 'What time have we got to be at the Hospital?' Stuart asks Tricia. 'Anytime after eleven they said.'

'Good that will give us time to get some of the jobs finished off from yesterday.' Stuart makes his tea with a tea bag in his mug, and stirs it round, as he looks up the garden, which is glowing in the morning sunshine. 'It looks like it's going to be another lovely day,' he says, as he turns round to see Tricia dashing upstairs from the kitchen having done her hair.

'Now where are you going?' Stuart asks. 'To make the beds, and get Claire up,' she shouts, as she ascends the stairs.

Stuart follows her up the stairs with his mug, and makes for the bathroom, and has his shave and shower before Claire gets up. Having got dressed into his old clothes, he decides to finish trimming the edges of the front lawn, which he had to stop suddenly the day before.

'Claire are you up yet?' Tricia asks as she walks across the landing towards Claire's bedroom. There is no reply. 'Now come on,' Tricia says, as she enters her room, 'I've got a lot on today Miss, and I need to get things done.' Claire stretches her arms up out of the bed covers and opens her eyes. 'What time is it?' she asks her mom. 'Its half past nine, now come on. I want to make your bed. Have you done all your packing?' Tricia asks. 'More or less,' Claire replies as she swings her legs out of bed, and puts her feet into her slippers, where she conveniently left them the night before.
Claire makes for the bathroom to have her shower, as Tricia makes her bed, and has a brief look at Claire's suitcase. My god, she thinks to herself, she has made

a good job of the packing, I am astounded, as she leaves her room, and returns to her own bedroom, and makes a start on their packing.

Packing suitcases is a meticulous job, and takes time to be done well, with things having to be put in, in the correct order. Mixed with some of Tricia's clothes and some of Stuart's, just in case one of the cases gets lost or damaged in the flight, it has been known for suitcases to go astray. The unimportant items are best put at the bottom of the case like beach towels, and shoes, and building up with trousers, and finally dresses and tops last. It takes time, and involves several hours' work, and there is no way it's going to be finished before they have to leave for the hospital.

Having had her shower and got dressed Claire enters her mother's bedroom. 'What time are you going to get Craig?' she asks. 'They said anytime after eleven. What time is it now?' Tricia asks. 'It's half past ten,' Claire replies. 'Well I suppose we will have to go. Where's your Dad?' 'I don't know, I suppose he's in the garden where he always is.' 'Be a love and gee him up will you?'

Claire walks over to the bedroom window of her mother's bedroom and opens it, and looks down, and sees her dad on his hands and knees picking weeds out of the front garden. 'Mom says come on we've got to get Craig from the Hospital.' A faint, 'Ok,' reply is heard, as Claire closes the window. 'He says Ok. Do you mind if I don't come with you to collect Craig?' 'No,' Tricia replies. 'Only I want to paint my toe nails, and I can have them done in peace without him hanging around.'

'Try and keep Suzie from wondering off will you. Only we will need to take her to the Kennels this afternoon.' 'I'll do my best,' Claire replies.

Having washed his hands and changed into more suitable clothes for the hospital, Stuart is ready. He is waiting in the kitchen, as Claire passes by with a pot of nail varnish in her hands, and makes for the garden. 'Are you coming to collect Craig?' Stuart asks her. 'No,' she replies. 'Charming, don't get too sunburnt will you,' Stuart remarks in a sarcastic tone. 'Leave her alone; she is going to paint her toenails while we're gone. Now come on,' Tricia says, as her comments caught Stuart by surprise, as he wasn't aware she was anywhere near.

They both leave the house and make their way to the hospital.

The hospital was very busy that morning, as they ride round and round the car park looking for a space. They eventually find a man walking towards his car, and they wait for him to reverse out so they can take his place. Having parked the car, they make their way into the hospital. It's very busy, and people seem to be everywhere. Visitors, patients and staff seemed to be coming from every direction, as they made their way along the corridors of the hospital towards the children's ward.

As they reach the children's ward the doors are locked, and they ring the bell, and wait for the door to be released to let them in. A buzzing noise is heard, and the door lock is released, and they open the door, and enter the ward. There are various rooms along the short corridor on both sides, as they walk towards the main ward infront of them.

Just prior to reaching the main ward, a nurse enters the corridor from a room on their right, and is about to enter the ward, and turns and sees Tricia and Stuart. It's a male nurse, and his badge says his name is Robert. 'Morning,' he says as they walk towards him. ' We've come to collect Craig Osborn, we are his Parents. How is he?' Tricia asks. 'Oh he's fine. The Doctor's seen him, and says he can go home when you're ready.' 'Thank God for that. Is it ok for him to fly tomorrow?' Tricia asks Robert. 'Yes, but just keep an eye on him, and let him have an early night to-night, and if you have any concerns while you are away just see a doctor, but I think he will be fine, he's a tough kid.'

'Well thanks for everything you have done for him.' 'That's alright.' 'So where is he then?' 'I think he's in the TV room playing with some of the other children.' Stuart and Tricia walk to the other end of the ward and see Craig playing with another boy on the computer. Tricia walks over to him. 'Mornin' Craig,' she says. He turns round, 'Hi Mom I'll only be a minute,' he says, as he carries on with his game. 'You will need to sign some papers, so call in the office on your way out will you,' Robert says, as he walks off to see another patient.

Craig finishes his game, and thanks the boy he was playing with. He walks towards his parents. 'How are you?' his mother asks, wishing to reassure herself everything is ok with him. 'I am fine, can we go home now?' 'Yes, but I have to sign some papers with Robert before we leave.' They find Robert, and Tricia signs the discharge papers, they all thank him and leave the ward.

On their way home, Craig tells his parents about one of the patients who was brought in badly hurt during the night, and the fact the commotion had kept him awake. 'Well you can have an early night tonight, and catch up on your sleep, because we have to be up early in the morning to catch the plane,' Tricia says. 'I can't wait for tomorrow,' Craig says as they reach their house.

They can all hear Max barking, as Stuart opens the back gate to enter the garden. Max is very pleased to see everyone back home and jumps up Craig, Craig gives him some fuss, as Max runs up the garden to bring his ball for Craig to throw for him.

'You're back then,' Claire says, as she looks up from the sun lounger.

'I thought they were going to keep you so we could have a good Holiday.' With that cutting remark Craig has Max's ball in his hand, and he can't resist the temptation, and instead of throwing it to Max, he aims it straight at Claire. He throws the ball, and hits his sister on the right shoulder. 'Ouch that hurt. You little sod you.' 'Oh, now stop it the pair of you.' 'Well she started it,' Craig replies. 'I don't care who started it just pack it in, I shan't tell you again,' Tricia says.

Having prepared the lunch, they all sit down to eat, afterwards Tricia carries on with the packing, while Stuart starts to gather the items of food for Suzy and Max, and packs them into a large cardboard box. He gets Max's lead and puts it on the kitchen work surface. Suzy's travelling basket is kept in the garage, and Stuart makes his way there to fetch it. He gives it a quick brush down and returns to the kitchen.

Now comes the problem where is the cat he thinks to himself. 'Has anyone seen Suzy?' he shouts, in the hope of someone answering.
'I think she's up here,' Tricia shouts from the bedroom.

Stuart goes upstairs. 'Where is she?' he asks Tricia, who is still packing their suitcases. 'She's on Claire's bed asleep as far as I know,' she replies. Stuart walks into Claire's room and there she is fast asleep on the bed. He reaches down and slowly strokes her in order not to frighten her. She slowly disturbs herself, and stretches her legs out as Stuart slips his hand gently under her and lifts her up. Gotcha he thinks to himself, that was easier than I thought it was going to be.
He takes her into Tricia. 'Say, bye, bye, to your Mummy.' Tricia gives Suzy's head a stroke. 'Have a nice Holiday,' Tricia says, as Stuart takes her down stairs, and puts her into her travelling basket. He'd already placed some of her toys inside, and her blanket. She looks round and sniffs the blanket, and meows her concerns as to what was happening to her.

Stuart takes Suzy and places her gently into the back of his Range Rover, and returns to the house to collect the food box, and Max's toys.

'Max, here boy,' Stuart shouts, as Max comes running in from outside.
Stuart clips his lead on his collar. 'Craig do you want to come to the Kennels with me?' Stuart shouts upstairs to him. 'Coming,' he replies as he bounds down the stairs. 'Take it steady,' Tricia shouts. 'Ok,' Craig replies. 'See you later,' Stuart shouts up to Tricia, as they leave the house.

Stuart opens the rear tailgate on the Range Rover, and Max jumps in, and sniffs Suzy's cage and lies down. He closes the tailgate; he and Craig get into the vehicle.

The journey to Farmhouse Kennels is about 5 miles from where they live. They leave town and travel along the bye pass past Bagley Hall Woods, and eventually turning right at the traffic island into Vassal Road and left into Farmhouse Kennels.

As they stop outside the office, Hanna one of the kennel maids is standing by the door. Both Craig and Stuart get out of the Range Rover, and walk towards the rear of the vehicle. 'It's Mr Osborn with Max and Suzy,' Stuart says. 'Oh yes, come on in, and we can sort things out. I'll be looking after them while you're away,' Hanna says, as they all enter the office.

Hanna walks over to the desk and opens the booking in book, and checks the days they are staying. 'It's fifteen nights isn't it?' Hanna asks Stuart. 'That's right,' he replies. 'That will be one hundred and ninety five pounds. How will you pay?' she asks. Stuart hands over his debit card. 'Will this be Ok?' 'That's fine,' Hanna replies, as she takes the card from him, and swipes it through her till.

'We're having some nice weather here at the moment, are you going anywhere exciting?' she asks. Craig butts in 'We're going on a plane to the Algarve,' he replies. 'Gosh that sounds nice,' Hanna says as the till starts to churn out the till receipt. She tears it off and hands it over to Stuart to sign.

'Well while you're away I will take good care of Max and Suzy for you,' Hanna says to Craig, who nods back in reply. 'Thanks,' Stuart says, as she hands him his receipt.

'Now let's go and get them settled in,' Hanna says to Craig as they leave the office. Stuart opens the tailgate, and Max jumps down, and jumps up Hanna for some fuss. 'Hello Max,' Hanna says, and gives his head a good rub. She takes hold of his lead, and guides him towards the kennels in the left hand corner of the yard, while Stuart takes Suzy out and follows Hanna. Other dogs can be heard barking and wagging their tails in excitement as they approach the entrance to the kennel block, all seeming to think their masters have come to collect them.

'Now I've put Max in room five next to a West Highland Terrier,' Hanna said, as they pass by the West Highland Terrier who was looking inquisitively at them. Hanna opens Max's door and guides him in. She releases his lead, and Max runs off straight through the trap door opposite the entrance into the open run. 'Well he doesn't seem to be a bit bothered about being here does he?' Hanna says to Craig. Max is already making friends with the West Highland Terrier as they sniff each other by the wire.

'Now lets get Suzy settled in,' Hanna says 'So follow me it's this way,' she adds and walks back towards the doorway, only this time they walk through another door into the cattery which is smaller and brighter than the dog section.

The little houses for the cats are about 1 metre wide with a door, which opens at about waist height. They are painted white with a built in light in the ceiling, with a litter tray in one corner, and a small basket in the other. Like the dog section they also have a trap door leading out to an exercise area, which is well off the ground, and has wire mesh on all sides, with a small tree branch and a rope hanging from the ceiling.

Stuart places Suzy's travelling basket on the floor, and opens the door and lifts her out, and places her into her little house. He gives her a stroke, as she cautiously looks around and sniffs the air in her strange new home. Hanna closes the door. 'There, she'll be all right won't she?' she says to Craig. 'I think so,' he says as Stuart picks up the travelling basket and they all leave the building.

'I've got all their food in the back of the car,' Stuart says, as they walk across the yard back towards the office.

Stuart opens the back of the Range Rover, and hands Hanna the food box along with Max's toys. He closes the door. 'Right, well thanks for everything, and we will see you in two weeks.' 'Yes, have a nice time,' Hanna says, as they drive off.

Chapter 14

Tricia is still packing the suitcases, as Stuart and Craig arrive back home.

'Hi we're back,' Stuart shouts upstairs as they enter the house. A faint hi reply is heard. Stuart puts the kettle on and makes his way up stairs to Tricia who is still in their bedroom. 'Hi love I've put the kettle on do you want a cup?' Stuart says. 'Yes I am dying for one,' Tricia replies. 'How are you doing?' 'Not too bad, but its tiring me out in this heat.' 'Well have a bit of a rest and come on down and have this cup of tea with me outside in the shade, and then 'ill give you a hand afterwards.'

Tricia didn't need asking twice as they both make their way down stairs. Tricia goes out into the garden, and sits on one of the patio chairs in the shade.

Stuart makes the tea and takes it outside to Tricia. 'Well how did it go with the animals then?' Tricia asks, as Stuart places the tea on the patio table. 'Ok, they seemed to settle in quickly. Max shot off out into his run to make friends with a West Highland Terrier next door, so he wasn't a bit bothered. Suzy was more cautious, but other than that she seemed ok.' 'Good,' Tricia replies.

They both enjoy their cup of tea and unwind in the shade. Claire is still on the sun lounger in her bikini. ' Are you all right?' Tricia asks Claire. 'Umm,' she says half dozing in the sunshine. 'You had better put some more lotion on madam,' Tricia says. 'She'll burn to death if she's not careful,' Tricia remarks to Stuart.

All is peaceful and quiet in the Osborn house as they relax in the warm summer afternoon.

However their peace is suddenly shattered with a very loud bang and crashing sound coming from upstairs. 'God, what the devil was that?' Tricia says.' 'I'd better go and find out,' Stuart remarks, as he makes his way upstairs in the direction of the noise.

As he reaches the landing he can hear what sounded like either moaning or a very faint chuckling sound coming from Craig's room.

'Are you alright Son?' Stuart asks, as he reaches the bedroom door, and looks inside to see a pair of legs sticking out of the built in wardrobe, with trousers around the ankles, and trainers on. As he got closer he could definitely make out it was Craig, and he could definitely make out laughter coming from the built in wardrobe.

'What the Devil have you done Son?' Stuart asks. In between the laughter he could just make out that he was trying to take his trousers off and over balanced, and fell into the wardrobe.'

With that Tricia comes rushing in. 'Is he alright?' she asks. 'Yes he's fine the silly sod was taking his trousers off, and over balanced, and fell into the wardrobe.' 'My God have you hurt yourself?' she asks, as she sees him still in the wardrobe, but trying to get up, and still laughing at himself. His laughter was very infectious, and soon they were all laughing at the predicament Craig had landed himself in.

'Come on,' Stuart says, 'Let's leave him to it, and finish this packing.'

Stuart and Tricia return to their bedroom and continue with the packing. 'I've put things in different cases so if one should get lost, we will still have some clothes,' Tricia says. 'You worry too much, nothings going to happen. They are very well organised these days,' Stuart remarks.

'Now shall I start to pack some of my shirts?' he asks Tricia. 'Yes that would be a big help, and I can carry on checking Craig's case.'

The evening wears on, the packing is done, and the evening meal has been eaten, and Tricia loads the dishwasher for the last time. 'I was just thinking, and looking at my 'To Do List' I wrote the other day,' Stuart says to Tricia. 'Have we got the First Aid Kit, Sun Tan Lotion, Insect Bite Cream, Mosquito Repellent, Sun Hats, Books to read, Sun Glasses and toilette needs?' 'Yes, except the Toilette Bag, as I shall need some things in the morning, but it's all ready to load in the case tomorrow as we leave,' she replies. 'Now what I want you to do is bring the Suitcases down here, so in the morning we've only to load them into the car as we leave,' Tricia says. With that Stuart makes his way upstairs.

'Craig,' Tricia shouts through to the lounge. 'Its nine o'clock I think you should be thinking about going to bed don't you?' 'Ok in a minute,' he replies. 'No... Now,' Tricia replies in a loud tone intending her comments to be obeyed, ' You will feel the benefit in the morning at half past three, so come on, move it.'

Craig grudgingly gets up off the sofa and makes his way upstairs, but gives his mom a kiss as he goes.

'I'll be up in a few minutes to tuck you in,' Tricia says. 'Oh no,' Craig replies under his breath so his mother wouldn't hear. 'I heard that,' Tricia says.

The kitchen door bangs open and Stuart enters with one of their suitcases, and places it on the dining room floor, and returns for the others.

Tricia goes upstairs to tuck Craig in. 'Now try and get some sleep, and have you got the clothes out for in the morning?' 'No,' he replies. 'Oh Craig as if I haven't got enough to do.' Tricia opens the wardrobe and takes a pair of blue tracksuit bottoms out and a white tee shirt, and a pair of white socks. His trainers were on the floor by his bed. 'Wear these in the morning, I'll leave them here on the door, and don't forget to put a clean pair of underpants on, do you hear?' 'Yes, stop fussing,' he replies, as he snuggles down under the duvet.

Tricia turns the light out as she leaves his room, and crosses the landing into Claire's room, and puts her head round the door. 'Everything all right in here?' 'Yes Mom,' Claire replies. 'Have you got the things out you are travelling in tomorrow?' Tricia asks. 'Yes,' Claire replies. 'Ok see you in the morning. I'll wake you,' Tricia says as she leaves the room.

She makes her way into her own bedroom, and starts to get ready for bed. Stuart follows her in and sets the alarm clock for 3 am, and tests it. A loud ringing is heard and he immediately switches it off, and resets it, and puts it on his bedside table. 'Where are the Tickets and Passports?' Tricia asks. 'They are all in the Dining Room, along with the Money, and Car Keys, and all the Hand Luggage, and the Suitcases.' 'Good,' Tricia replies, as Stuart gets into bed, and turns his bedside light out.

Tricia goes to the bathroom and returns about 10 minutes later, and gets into bed, and turns her light out.

She lies there with her eyes wide open, and Stuart is lying on his side facing away from her.

'I hope we don't have any problems on the Plane,' Tricia says to Stuart. 'Such as?' he replies. 'Well, I don't know do I.' 'What do you think is going to happen?' 'Well, what if it crashes.' 'Now you are being silly.' 'Planes do crash.' 'I know, but flying is the safest means of transport in the world. We are more likely to get killed going to the airport than on the flight. So stop worrying and go to sleep.'

Tricia lies there in the dark still not at peace with her mind over flying, but eventually she falls asleep.

Not only do passengers need a good nights sleep, but also flight crews, particularly when they are on an early flight. Senior flight attendant Zoe Hammond is a stewardess for Air Five Thousand, and has been for the last five years. During this time she has also managed to juggle raising a young family with her husband Andrew, who is a chartered accountant for a large midland firm. Evening time is very busy for her, and she tries to get the early shifts where she can, as she can leave the nanny to attend to the children in the morning, as Andrew goes off to work.

'Come on Laura into those pyjamas please, and be quick about it. Beth have you cleaned your teeth?' Zoe shouts to her eldest daughter who is eight years old, and very grown up for her age. 'Can you read me a story please?' Laura asks her mom. 'Yes go and pick a book you want.'

Laura is nearly four with bright blue eyes and blonde hair, and a china dolls face. She has a lovely personality and speaks beautifully for her age. She selects her favourite book from the bookcase in her bedroom, and climbs into bed, and wriggles down under the duvet, and hands the book to her mom.

Zoe commences reading the story to Laura who eventually falls asleep. She slowly tucks her hands under the cover of the duvet and turns the light out as she creeps out of her room.

She crosses the landing and checks on the baby of the family, James who is just twelve months old, and is asleep in his cot in the nursery with his left leg stuck up in the air, and resting against the bars of his cot. She thinks she had better leave him alone as she creeps out and enters Beth's room. Beth has a bunk bed, and she is lying wide-awake and reading a book. 'Don't be long will you; you have school in the morning. Have you got your things ready?' 'Yes,' she says to her mom. 'I am just going down stairs to your Dad, and when I come up I want you asleep, and that light off.' 'Ok,' Beth replies, as she carries on reading. Zoe gives her head a kiss as she leaves the room.

'They're all in bed', Zoe says to Andrew, who is watching TV, and makes no reply, as she enters the kitchen and finishes clearing up from dinner. Andrew follows her, and puts his arms around her waist as she finishes some washing up. He kisses her neck. 'Where are you off to tomorrow?' he asks. 'Faro in Portugal, and I should be back by tea time at the latest.' 'What time will you be going out?' 'About five.' 'Don't wake me will you'? 'Now you know I won't, I never do.' 'Well I had better get what nibbles I can now then,' as he kisses her neck and gives it a loving bite.

She has soapsuds on her hands and plonks some on his face. 'Arr that's yuck, but if that's what you want.' He grabs at a handful of soapsuds and throws them at her, as she runs squealing from the kitchen into the lounge, and dives onto the settee laughing and giggling. Andrew dives on top of her and they kiss each other. 'I love you,' he says. 'I know, and I love you too, but this isn't getting the washing up done, and I want an early night remember.' She pushes him off, and he rolls onto the floor. She gets up and dashes back into the kitchen. Andrew rolls over and watches the TV from the floor as Zoe finishes off the washing up, and walks through to the lounge. 'Well I am off. You can switch everything off when you come up.' She makes her way upstairs to the bathroom, and then she checks on Beth, to see if she has turned her light off, but she hasn't, she has fallen asleep, so she turns off the light, and closes the door behind her.

Having got undressed and into bed, she turns out her bedside light, setting her alarm for four thirty, giving herself time to get up and get dressed, and out by five o'clock. Andrew quietly enters the bedroom, and gets undressed, and snuggles up to Zoe, and they soon fall asleep.

Chapter 15

Both Tricia and Stuart have a restless nights sleep with one or the other tossing and turning.

Stuart opens his eyes and looks up at the ceiling to see the time, which is projected onto the ceiling by the time projection clock, showing the time in a red glow as 01.33. God, he thinks to himself is that all the time is, I feel as if I have been to sleep for days.

He closes his eyes and eventually falls to sleep again and starts to dream.

Ringggggggggggggggggggggg. Ringgggggggggggggggggggggg its 3 am and the alarm clock wakes them both up, and Stuart reaches over still half asleep, and hits the alarm clock, and switches it off. He immediately swings his legs out of bed, and yawns, and stretches his arms out, 'Mornin' love, can I go to the Bathroom first?' he asks Tricia. 'Yes, I'll wake the kids,' she replies.

They both get out of bed, and leave the bedroom. Stuart goes to the bathroom, and Tricia goes first into Craig's room. He is still fast asleep. In order not to startle him, she reaches down and gently strokes his head. 'Mornin,' love it's time to get up,' she leans down and gives his forehead a kiss. Craig slowly wakes up, and stretches his arms and nods his head to his mother. 'Your Dad has just gone to the Bathroom, and then I am going in, so just slowly wake yourself,' she says.

She then enters Claire's room. Her bedside light is on, and she is lying on her side. She raises her arm, and waves to her mother acknowledging the fact she is awake. 'I am just going to the Bathroom, and then you can go,' Tricia says, and Claire waves her arm again, but still not speaking.

'It's all yours love,' Stuart says as he exits the bathroom and re-enters the bedroom, and starts to get dressed.

He throws the duvet cover over the bed, and fluffs up the pillows in order to leave the bed tidy while they are away. He partially opens the bedroom curtains, and has a look at the weather outside. It's another fine dry morning, and dawn will soon be breaking.

He makes his way down stairs and switches the kettle on. Despite the fact they are about to leave on holiday, he is determined he is not leaving the house without his morning cup of tea.

Tricia gathers her toiletries up in the bathroom, and makes for her bedroom, and puts her head round the door into Craig's room. 'Ok you can go now.' He jumps out of bed, and runs across the landing to the bathroom half singing, 'We are going on Holiday.' Tricia gets dressed, and starts to put her make up on. She hears Craig has finished. 'Go and tell Claire she can go now.' He rushes into Claire's room, and dives on her bed. 'Get up lazy bones we're going on Holiday,' 'Get off, and clear off,' she says, as she gets out of bed, as Craig makes a dash for his room.

Stuart walks into the dining room, and picks up his car keys, puts them into his trouser pocket along with his wallet. He then picks up the currency, and flight tickets, and puts them into his lightweight travelling flight bag, which is draped over one of the dining chairs. It also contains their reading books, a bottle of water and a small packet of biscuits, which he has just removed from the fridge as a last minute thought. He also sees he has his sunglasses. He picks up the passports and counts them one by one to make sure he has all four, which of course he has, and he puts them into the flight bag. I won't forget those now will I, he thinks to himself.

He partially opens the dining room blinds and walks through to the lounge, and does the same.

He returns to the kitchen, and finishes his cup of tea, as Tricia walks in. 'Do you want a cup of tea?' he asks. 'No thanks; I will wait until we get to the Airport. Can you put this in the Suitcase for me?' she asks, as she hands Stuart her toilette bag. He reaches down and opens the case, puts it in and relocks it, and sets the combination lock on the handle. 'That's bound to make it over,' he says in a joking manner.
'I do hope not!' Tricia replies.

They both hear Craig running down the stairs, and making one hell of a racket as he does so. Tricia turns towards the hall door as Craig comes bounding in. 'Quiet, you noisy little devil you will wake the whole street up. Is Claire up?' she asks Craig. 'No she is still in bed,' 'No I'm not I'm getting dressed,' she shouts down from her bedroom.

Stuart makes a start in loading the suitcases into the car. He picks one of the cases up and staggers through to the front door. 'Can I help?' Craig asks. 'Yes you can open the door for me.' Craig turns the front door key, and opens the door, and follows his father outside. He had never been up and out so early in his life, and this was quite an adventure, even a little scary in the dark, as everywhere was so quiet. Stuart reaches into his pocket, and gets his car keys out, and opens the Range Rover, and lowers the door, and throws the suitcase in.

'Can I get the other suitcases?' Craig asks his father. 'You can carry the little one. 'Ok,' he says, as he rushes back into the house to fetch it.

Stuart follows Craig back into the house and picks the other two heavy cases up, and returns to the Range Rover, and places them in the boot. Craig places his little case on the tailgate for his father to place in the back properly. 'Right that just leaves the main Flight Bag with the Passports to pick up,' he says to Craig, as he closes the tailgate quietly.

Stuart and Craig re-enter the house and Stuart looks at his watch. It's 03.26 am. 'Are we all ready?' he asks Tricia. 'No, we're just waiting for Claire,' she says. Stuart finishes his cup of tea, and washes the cup under the tap, and replaces it in the cupboard. Tricia disconnects the kettle from the mains, and wipes the sink unit down.

They both hear footsteps coming down the stairs, and Claire enters the
kitchen. 'Have you made your bed and opened your curtains?' Tricia asks her.
'No,' she replies. 'Well go on back up and do them please.'
'No one is going to see anything.' 'I don't care, go and do as I have asked please, and have you done yours Craig?' 'No.' 'Well go and do yours as well, and don't be long either of you.' They both go upstairs to do as they have been asked. Tricia gives Stuart one of her looks that could kill a horse at a thousand paces.

'Right, just the Flight Bag now,' Stuart reaches down and picks it up. 'I'll have it in the front with me,' Tricia says as she takes the bag from him.

Claire and Craig re-enter the kitchen. 'All done,' Tricia says, 'that didn't hurt did it?' There was no response from the children. 'Have you got everything you need with you in your satchels?' Tricia asks them both. 'Yes,' they reply. 'Right lets go then,' Stuart says as they all leave the house. He sets the alarm, and locks the front door.

Chapter 16

The family drive through the town on their way towards the motorway. All is quiet, not a living soul about, the street lights are on. Everywhere has an eerie appearance, as if everyone has left town, and they are the only humans left in existence.

Stuart gathers speed as he drives along the dual carriageway towards the motorway, passing a lorry as he climbs the hill.

The motorway is busy even at 3.30 am with night freight truckers travelling through the night with parcels to various destinations.

Stuart looks in his interior mirror and sees Craig has nodded off to sleep. He whispers to Tricia, 'He's asleep already.' Tricia turns round and smiles.

He turns off the M5 motorway and enters the M42 motorway for the airport. He looks at his speedometer, which registers just under 70 m.p.h, as he travels along lane one.

Dawn is just about breaking as they travel eastwards towards the airport. This section of motorway is deserted, and it is a very pleasant experience to travel on in the early hours of the day.

Looking into his offside wing mirror he sees a pair of headlights behind him in the middle lane, gaining on his vehicle.

'It looks like it's going to be another lovely day weather wise,' he says to Tricia. 'I do hope so,' she replies.

Suddenly the vehicle in the middle lane overtakes their vehicle. It's a dark coloured 4x4, which is towing a caravan.

'God he must be doing eighty plus with that thing on the back,' Stuart remarks, as the vehicle remains in the middle lane, and pulls away in the distance.

'He should only be doing sixty, not eighty plus, he'll come a cropper if he doesn't slow down,' Stuart says.

'Well that will be his problem, there's no need for you to get stressed by it,' Tricia replies.

They start to climb a hill and the 4x4 has gone over the top and out of sight as they travel along still doing just under 70 m.p.h.

They eventually reach the top of the hill and start to descend. Stuart can see the taillights on the caravan way, way, in the distance still in the middle lane. However they seem to be swinging from side to side, but it's difficult to see as there are no streetlights on this section of motorway.

Suddenly they swing towards the central barrier, and then back towards the middle lane, and then the lights go vertical, sparks can be seen flying into the air, then the lights go out, and the sparks stop.

'It's crashed,' Stuart shouts. 'Oh my God,' Tricia says, and puts her hand to her mouth. 'What's happened?' Claire says. 'There has been an accident, a caravan has overturned,' Stuart says.

They eventually arrive at the scene. Stuart stops on the hardshoulder, and puts his hazard lights on. Fortunately he stopped near to an emergency phone. 'Go and phone the Police from the phone,' Stuart says to Tricia. 'Where are we?' 'I don't know, but the Police will from the phone.'

He gets out of the vehicle, and goes to the back, and gets out his torch.
He looks back up the motorway, there's no one coming, so he runs out into the carriageway, and goes to the overturned vehicle with it's nearside wheels slowly turning round in the air.

Tricia opens the door to the phone box and picks up the receiver, and hears the phone ringing in the earpiece. It seems ages until someone answers. 'Hello Police, can I help?' the voice says. 'Yes there's been an accident just in front of this phone, a car and caravan have overturned in the middle lane,' Tricia says. 'Has anyone been hurt?' the operator asks. 'I don't know, my husband has just gone to look?' Tricia replies. 'Are you involved?' 'No we just saw it happen.' The operator asks for her name and address and telephone number. 'We're just going to the airport on holiday,' Tricia remarks to the operator.

Stuart passes the underside of the 4x4 as it lies on its offside, and walks round the front of the vehicle towards the roof. Just on that the glass sunroof panel opens and falls to the ground. The driver is just starting to climb out of the hole.

Stuart reaches down and offers the driver a hand to assist him out. 'Are you all right?' Stuart asks. 'I think so,' the driver replies, as he gets to his feet. Stuart puts his arm around the driver. 'Come on we must get to the hardshoulder.' Stuart and the driver make it to the hardshoulder, Stuart sits the man down. 'Do you want to go to hospital?' he asks. 'No I'll be all right in a minute,' he says.

With that Stuart makes for Tricia and the phone. 'Is he all right?' Tricia asks. 'Yes, he says he doesn't want to go to hospital.'

Stuart looks back along the motorway and sees headlights coming towards them. He switches his torch on, and starts to run back along the hardshoulder passed his Range Rover swinging the torch as he goes, to warn the approaching traffic of the accident.

The lights move towards the middle lane, and then Stuart hears a skidding sound, and realises the vehicle is braking very hard. It swings across into the third lane, and hits the central crash barrier. It bounces back into the middle lane, still skidding. It then starts to swing round, and hits the back of the caravan. There is a terrific explosion as the caravan is torn apart by the impact.

Tricia screams down the phone to the operator. 'What's happened now?' the operator asks. 'Someone has just hit the caravan, and it has blown up. My God you had better come quickly.' 'We are on our way, and the Fire Brigade will also be attending,' the operator says, as Tricia puts the phone down and slams the door shut, and runs back to their Range Rover. Debris is falling from the sky like snowflakes all round them, but there is no fire or smoke.

Stuart realises the vehicle which hit the caravan is a white Ford Transit Van. The driver gets out with a cut to his head, and blood running down his face.

The driver staggers as he walks towards them and the hardshoulder, wiping his face with a hankie. At the same time Stuart sees headlights coming over the brow of the hill towards them, but they are different, and they are flashing, and then he sees a blue light amongst them. Thank God it's the police he thinks to himself.

'Come here mate, I have a First Aid Kit in the back.' Stuart opens the tailgate and reaches into the back, and attends to the mans cut forehead.

The Police Range Rover stops short of the scene. One policeman goes to the back of the Range Rover and gets a stack of cones out, and runs back along the carriageway with them. The driver approaches Stuart 'What happened?' he asks. 'The 4x4 and caravan overturned, and the driver is sitting over there, and then this van crashed into the back of it.' Stuart says. The policeman goes back to his police car and radios back asking for lanes 3 and 2 closure on the central matrix signals. His colleague has already started to cone off the offside lane across towards the first lane.

The cut to the van driver's head seemed quite severe at first, but after Stuart's first aid attention isn't too bad, as he puts a plaster across the cut and manages to stop the bleeding. 'I think you'll be all right now, but if it bleeds again you might want to see a Doctor,' Stuart says to the driver. 'No I am sure it will be ok. Thanks,' he says.

The driver of the police car approaches Stuart and the van driver with his clip board in order to take details. Stuart says to him, 'We are just off to the airport to catch a plane to Portugal. We have given our details to the operator, can we go, and if you need anything more we will be back in two weeks?' 'Yes, thanks for all your help,' the policeman says.

Stuart walks away from the van driver, and beckons the policeman towards him. In a quiet voice he says, 'The driver of the 4x4 passed me at well over eighty, and I think he has been drinking.' 'Ok,' the policeman says.

Stuart and Tricia get into their Range Rover, and leave the scene.

'God that was close,' Tricia remarks to Stuart. 'Are you kids all right in the back?' Stuart asks. 'Yeah, that was brill Dad. Boom, better than on the Tele,' Craig replies.

'You were very brave Dad,' Claire says. 'My Dads a hero,' Craig says.

'Let's hope nothing else happens?' Tricia says. 'What's the time?' Stuart asks. 'It's five past four,' Tricia replies.

Chapter 17

'How much further?' Tricia asks Stuart. 'It's not far, only about another couple of miles,' he replies.

Stuart is mindful of the time in which he has to be at the airport in order to check in for the flight, but he still feels they will have plenty of time to get parked up and into the terminal building.

He is still travelling at 70 m.p.h. and making good progress due to the sparseness of traffic at this time of the day. They have all calmed down after the accident and are relaxed as the radio is on and the music is playing softly. They pass the junction sign for the airport, 1mile to go.

As they pass the sign Stuart sees an old car broken down on the hardshoulder, and a very smartly dressed young man pacing up and down near the rear of the car. As he drives by the man looks at him, as if to ask if he could help. Stuart slows down, and pulls up on the hardshoulder.

'What's up now?' Tricia asks. 'I think that guy back there needs a lift, I am just going back to see if I can help.' 'Oh no, we will never get to the airport at this rate,' Tricia says, as Stuart reverses his Range Rover back towards the broken down car.

Stuart stops short of the vehicle, and the driver approaches the passenger side of his Range Rover, and Tricia opens her window and turns the radio off.

The man is very handsome Tricia thinks to herself, he has short black hair and he is in his early thirties. He is wearing a smart uniform and cap, and a gold braid ring on the cuffs of each sleeve of his jacket.

Stuart leans across Tricia. 'What up mate?' 'I've run out of petrol, and I need to get to the airport as quick as possible,' the man says.

Stuart gets out of his Range Rover and the man walks to the back of his vehicle.

'Would you like a tow to the all night garage just off the junction?' Stuart asks the man. 'Please, I would be most grateful,' he replies, as Stuart starts to get his tow rope out of the back of his Range Rover, and attaches it to the towing hitch on the front of the car.

'Have you ever been towed before?' Stuart asks. 'No,' he replies. 'Well the thing is, to release your handbrake, and put the car into neutral gear, and switch the ignition on. I will only be going very slowly, and if we go down a gradient put your brakes on slightly, just to keep the rope torte, and release the brakes when we go up hill. Got that?' 'Yes, I think so,' the man replied.

They both get back into their cars and Stuart moves off slowly. 'Where are we going now?' Tricia asks. 'There's an all night petrol station just round the corner, we have to pass it on our way to the airport, and this guy needs our help.'

'Yes fair enough, but will he help us if we miss our flight?' Tricia asks. 'Oh stop whinging, we won't miss the flight.'

Stuart slowly makes his way off the motorway, and turns towards the airport along the dual carriageway, and pulls into the all night petrol station, and stops close enough to a petrol pump for the guy to fill up.

He unhitches the towrope from the vehicles and puts it back into the Range Rover.

'Thanks ever so much, you have saved my day,' the man replies.

'So what do you do for a living?' Stuart asks, knowing full well what the man did, as from his appearance he was a pilot with an airline. 'I am a First Officer with Air 5000, and I am due to take a flight to Portugal this morning.' 'Well, now there's a coincidence,' Stuart remarks, 'So are we, and oh dear, who didn't do his Cock Pit drill this morning before he set off.' 'Oh I know it is so embarrassing,' he replied. 'Well I hope you don't forget to do it on the plane.' 'I know don't remind me.' They both laugh as he continues to put petrol into his car.

'Is there anything I can do for you?' the man asked. 'Well now, I just love flying. I have flown a Cessna 152, and I have my own Flight Simulator at home, and I have flown other Flight Simulators as well,' Stuart remarked. 'So I suppose a visit to the Cock Pit on our flight this morning might go down well?' the man replied.

'By heck it wouldn't half, and my young Son would also be thrilled to bits if that's ok.' Stuart said. 'I will see what I can do for you. What's your name?' 'Stuart Osborn,' 'I am John Cutler, and if things go to plan I will call you on the planes PA to come up front. Will that be ok?' 'Yes that will be fine,' Stuart replied in a state of bewildered shock of the luck he had just had.

John finishes filling his car up with petrol and goes to pay. 'Can I suggest you try and start the engine, because if it won't start I can give you a tow,' Stuart says. 'Oh yes ok,' John replies, as he gets in and turns the ignition. The engine turns over several times before it catches and runs normally. He revs it up a few times and all seems well. 'That's fine I will leave you to it then,' Stuart says.

90

'Thanks a lot,' John replies, and makes his way to the all night kiosk to pay for the petrol.

Stuart gets into the Range Rover and fastens his seat belt. 'Come on we're going to be late,' Tricia says. 'Don't worry my dear we won't miss the plane, because that was the Pilot we have just helped.' ' Oh my God never.' 'Yes, and by way of a thank you he has invited us up into the Cock Pit when we are on our way to Faro.' 'What me as well?' Craig asks in an excited and hopeful manner. 'Yes you as well.' ' Wow wait 'til I tell them at school.'

The whole family seems very excited at the prospects of seeing the flight deck from the air as they reach the long stay car park. Stuart opens the window, and pulls the ticket from the machine as the barrier goes up, and they drive through. 'Now look for a suitable space that will take this thing,' he asks Tricia, as he drives round following the directional arrows. The car park seems full and there are no spaces near to the entrance, and they go deeper into the car park. 'There are two spaces together over there,' Tricia points to her right. 'Oh yes, that will take us,' Stuart replies and turns into the bay and parks straight.

The bus collection stop is only a few feet away, and Stuart sees the transfer bus on the far side of the car park making its way towards them. 'Come on let's get these bags out quick, the bus is on its way.'

'Shall I go to the bus stop and make sure it waits for us?' Craig asks. 'Yes and you take a bag and go with him Claire.' Claire grabs her bag and Craig's, and they both run towards the bus stop. Stuart and Tricia grab a suitcase each, and Tricia makes towards the bus wheeling the suitcase along by the handle, as Stuart locks the car up, and makes his way towards them, just as the bus pulls up.

Claire and Craig get on and walk down the bus, and place their suitcases in the rack as Stuart and Tricia join them.

As there are people already on the bus it doesn't stop again until it reaches the main terminal. They all start to get off. 'I'll go and get a trolley,' Craig says. Stuart makes his way to get the suitcases from the rack and gets off the bus. Craig pushes the trolley towards them, and Stuart loads the suitcases on to it.

They make their way into the terminal looking for Air 5000 flight checking in desk for Faro. Stuart sees it, desk 18 and flight number MAM 275. 'It's over there,' and they make their way over to the right and join a short queue for the desk.

Tricia gets the flight tickets and passports out of the flight bag ready to be checked.

They eventually reach the desk and hand in their tickets and passports. The young checking in clerk is very smartly dressed in her flight attendants uniform. She is about 21 years old, with blonde hair, and blue eyes. How do they pick these girls, they are all alike, slim gorgeous looking, with blonde hair, and blue eyes, Stuart thinks to himself.

'Please place the cases on the belt,' she says. 'Have you packed them yourself?' 'Yes,' Tricia replies. 'Are there any hair sprays or other inflammable or electrical devices in them?' 'No.' 'Would you like smoking or non smoking?' 'Non smoking please.'

'Window seats if possible,' she adds. ' Yes you will have three one side of the isle and one on the other side. Will that be all right?' 'Yes that will be fine.' 'You will be in row 20 seats A B C D.' The flight assistant puts the baggage labels onto the suitcases and hands the boarding passes and passport to Tricia. 'Go up to the departure lounge and watch the TV screens for your boarding times.' 'Thank you,' Tricia says, as they move away from the checking in desk.

They walk across the main foyer towards the escalator to the first floor, and round to the entrance to the departure lounge.

This is the main security checking area. A security lady in her late thirties asks them to place their bags onto the conveyer belt, which one by one they do, and watch them disappear into the machine.

'Would you put any keys or other metal objects into this basket and put them onto the belt as well,' the security lady says. Stuart empties his pocket of his car keys and his wallet, which has coins in, and places them into a basket. 'Would you all please walk through the x-ray arch,' the security lady asks. Craig goes first, and then Claire, and Tricia, and finally Stuart. They all get a green light.

However as they go to collect their bags the security lady watches them and sees Tricia pick her flight bag up. 'Is this your bag madam?' the security lady asks. 'Yes, why?' Tricia asks as her heart sinks lower. Oh my God what has she found she thinks to herself, as the adrenaline starts to pump as she becomes anxious as to what the lady has spotted in her bag?

'Would you mind opening it?' 'No.' Tricia opens the bag, and the security lady looks inside and asks her. 'What's in there?' She points to a clear plastic freezer bag with white powder inside. Tricia reaches in and picks the bag out. 'You mean this?' 'Yes,' the security lady replies. 'It's washing powder. I put it in my bag as I forgot to pack it into the case as we were leaving. Do you want to check it?' 'No I believe you.' 'You can if you like,' Tricia says. 'No I trust you,' she says.

Tricia was so embarrassed as everyone behind her seemed to be looking at her, as she puts the washing powder back in the bag, and closes it.

'What was all that about?' Stuart asks, as they walk away. 'They wanted to see what that white powder was in my bag,' she said in as quiet a tone as she could, not wishing to be overheard. 'I told them it was washing powder, which of course it is.' 'Why didn't you put it in the suitcase?' 'It was a last minute thought to take some just in case.'

'Never mind,' Stuart replies. 'It's all right for you to say never mind, but I feel so embarrassed.' 'Oh, don't be silly.' 'I shan't do that again in a hurry.'

They carry on walking towards the cafeteria. 'Can we have something to eat?' Craig asks. 'Yes we are all having some breakfast,' Tricia replies. 'Good I am starving,' Craig says, as he makes his way into the seating area. They find a table which is free, and not far from the window, and they place their bags on the floor. 'Now what does everyone want?' 'I'll have toast and coffee please,' Tricia replies. 'Claire what do you want?' 'I'll have the same please.' 'Craig,' 'Can I come and choose something?' 'Yes Ok.' 'Do you want a hand?' Tricia asks. 'No it's all right I can manage,' as he and Craig make their way to the food area. 'Get two trays will you Craig,' as they make their way along the line.

Most airlines have their own offices in most airports, for the flight crews to deal with pre-flight preparations. The offices log flight plans order fuel and food for the flights and sort out flight crew rosters and many administration duties required with all aspects of flying in a modern world.

It is where all flight crews usually report for duty, ensuring they obtain all the necessary information they require for the flights they are scheduled to go on. Flight attendants check all aspects of catering including the drinks order, and the number of passengers on both the out going and return flights. The flight crews check baggage loads, passenger numbers, and fuel loads in relation to both these items, weather forecasts for the departure point, and the destination.

The duty officer manager has to ensure all the crews for each flight is on duty well before the flight is due out. Because if anyone is missing, then arrangements have to be made to get replacements as quick as possible, so as not to cause a delay in the flight, which could cost the company vast amounts of money.

The duty flight manager today is getting concerned about the lateness of the First Officer for flight MAM two seven five for Faro, who hasn't reported for duty, and he is over half an hour late.

'Has anyone seen John Cutler?' he shouts to anyone in the office who may have an inkling as to why he is late. There was a deathly silence.

'Have you seen him Martin?' he asks. Martin is the captain on flight MAM two seven five who is looking at the weather charts on the front desk. 'No, but you know he has that beat up old car. It's probably conked out on him.' 'Or he's run out of petrol,' someone shouted from the back of the office, which causes a few sniggers from the flight attendants.

With that, the office door opens and in walks John the lost flight crewmember. 'Good morning, sorry I'm late had a bit of bother with the car.' 'What did you do run out of petrol?' someone shouted from the back of the office. John looked very sheepish at the remark and started to blush with embarrassment, as his leg was being pulled, and his sins were now being well and truly exposed.

'Yes he did,' someone shouted as the laughter broke out in the room. 'Just look at that guilty look on his face.'

'Ok I plead guilty. The wife had it last and never put any petrol in it,' he says. 'It's no good blamin' your misses mate. Just make sure we have enough gas to get to Faro,' someone shouted as the laughter grew even louder.

By now John realised there was no way they were going to let it drop. So for the sake of his own dignity, he might as well surrender, and keep his mouth shut so as not to make things worse.

He makes his way over to Martin. 'Sorry about that,' he says. 'Oh don't worry about it, you know what they are like, they just love to take the piss when they can. By the way I have checked the fuel load sheets up to now.'

Both Martin and John settle down to check over the weather charts and flight plans together, before they make their way to the aircraft.

Chapter 18

'What's the time Mom?' Claire asks Tricia. 'Ten past five,' she replies. 'We haven't done too bad considering the events so far today have we?' Claire remarks. 'No, and we should have time for breakfast and a look round the duty free shop before we have to board the plane. They should start boarding about six thirty I reckon,' Tricia says, as she looks around the cafeteria for Stuart. 'Where the devil are they?' she asks.

'Here they come,' Claire says, as she sees Craig leading the way with a tray of drinks and food.

'What kept you?' she asks Stuart, who has just reached the table with his tray of food. 'We had to wait for toast, the machine was slow, and there was a queue, and this young man here couldn't make his mind up whether to have Rice Crispies or Coco Pops.'

They settle down to enjoy their breakfast.

Tricia looks at her watch. It's twenty to six. 'Can we have a look round the duty free shop?' she asks Stuart. 'Yes are we all done?' he asks, but he gets no reply, but everyone gets up from the table having tidied everything onto one tray. Stuart picks the tray up and takes it to the return tray trolley on the far side of the cafeteria.

They make their way to the duty free shop by the main waiting area. 'You girls go on; I am going to check the boarding time. I know where to find you,' he says to Tricia, as Tricia and Claire make for the shop.

Stuart wanders across to a boarding screen and sees their flight listed MAM 275 towards the bottom, with no time or gate number as yet.

'Can we go and look at the planes Dad?' Craig asks, and starts to make his way towards the big windows overlooking the parking area for the planes. Stuart joins him by the window, and sees small tug vehicles towing several trailers loaded with suitcases, snaking their way across the tarmac. Petrol tankers can also be seen with their yellow flashing lights on, filling the planes with fuel. The area is very busy, with people and vehicles moving around in different directions.

Stuart recognises a white plane with a blue tailfin with Air 5000 on it. It's a Boeing 737, and a man in pilots uniform can be seen walking round the plane checking the air intakes, and the wheels, and wings. He recognises the man as John Cutler the pilot he helped earlier. He leans down to Craig and whispers in his ear.

'See that man down there walking round the plane, well that's the man I helped, and it would appear that's the plane we will be going on.' 'Gosh can I go and tell Mom?' He turns round and makes for the duty free shop to tell his mother he has seen the plane they will be flying on.

Stuart watches for a little while longer, and then walks back towards the boarding screens to see if their flight number has moved up the screen, but there was still no boarding time or gate number and he continues towards the duty free shop.

He finds Tricia and Claire looking at perfume and trying different testing bottles. As he approaches them Tricia looks up and sees him.

'Hi love, can I have a bottle of this Anais Anais please?' 'Yes if you like,' Stuart replies. Claire is browsing through various lipsticks and opens an orange coloured one. 'Do you think this will suit me Mom?' she asks. 'Yes I think so.' 'Can I have it then please?' she asks in a pleading way. 'I should think so,' Tricia replies.

Stuart heads for the alcohol area and starts looking at the whisky bottles, and he can't believe how cheap they are compared to the high street prices. He picks up a bottle of Grouse whisky, it's only a half bottle of whisky, but it's plenty he thinks to himself as he joins Tricia and Claire. 'What have you got there?' Tricia asks, as she looks at the bottle of whisky in his hand.

'Oh it's just something for your Mom when we get back. I know she likes a tipple or two with her nightcap. Are we all spent up now?' Stuart asks Tricia 'Yes I think so.' So they make their way to the check out desk to pay for their goods.

They all wander across to the main waiting area and sit down on the seats along with other passengers waiting for their flights.

Stuart looks around and sees there are other moms and dads, some with young children being nursed by their mothers, as they try and get a little sleep after their routine sleep pattern has been disrupted. For most of them it must be an anxious time, and possibly their first time on a plane. Their parents will be used to the routine, but not these little ones, who not only have been taken from their beds, but also are shortly to be put on a noisy plane and thrust into the air at great speed. It will be a frightening experience, and there are bound to be tears. Even some adults don't like flying, let alone young children.

Stuart reflects to himself on his first flight, and how apprehensive he was by it all, but he still enjoyed the journey to Gatwick from Birmingham all those years ago, and now he wishes he could do it everyday, as he just loves flying.

Stuart was sitting next to a couple in their early forties. The lady was dressed in terracotta coloured lightweight slacks, and a pale orange coloured tee shirt. The man was wearing beige coloured casual trousers, and a light green tee shirt. They both seemed very pleasant people and very sociable. The lady turns to Stuart and said.

'Where are you flying to?' 'We're off to Faro in Portugal.' 'Oh so are we,' she turns to her husband and passes the information onto him.

'Have you been before?' she asks. 'No,' Stuart replies. 'Have you?' he adds.

'No, and I have never flown before, and I didn't even know I was coming until we arrived at the airport.' 'Oh my God,' Stuart replies.

He turns to Tricia and tells her about the couple next to him. The lady then adds, 'It's a surprise holiday from my Husband.' 'Well I never. Are you ok about it?' 'I guess I will have to be, but I am not looking forward to the flight.' 'Ah, you will be all right. Flying is the safest means of transport, and it is so exciting you will love it. I just hope we haven't got an outside toilet on this flight.' They all burst out laughing.

Stuart seemed quite pleased with himself, as he had eased the atmosphere with the couple next to them.

Looking round the waiting area gave him time to do some people watching, like the lady opposite with two small girls. He estimated their ages as about 8 and 4 years old. Both girls had blonde hair and blue eyes. There didn't seem to be a man with them, but they seemed happy enough, and were very well behaved. He thought to himself I wonder what the reason is for their journey, and I wonder where they are going.

He also sees two elderly couples sitting next to each other opposite him, and the men are reading newspapers. He tries to read the headlines without being noticed, and slightly turning his head very slowly to one side to make them out, but the page is too creased to see what it says.

One of the ladies with them, who was wearing glasses, and dressed in pale blue slacks, and a white blouse, is talking to the lady next to her. She must have been the wife of the bald headed man reading the paper, as she occasionally glanced in his direction. He looked like a real miserable old git, and gave the impression he would rather be somewhere else. Stuart could just about make out the conversation the two ladies were having with each other, but the lady in the glasses seemed to be in command of the story she was telling.

'Yes I know, there seems so much of it about. It's a dirty habit, and despite what they say, people still keep on doing it. Do you know, a friend of mine had five operations to remove tumours from her bladder, and then they still had to remove it? They say it was caused by passive smoking. You know, inhaling other people's smoke. She had never smoked in her life. It's terrible. Fancy having to go through all that just because of other people's pleasure. What pleasure is in that, when her husband has to help her change her Stoma bag every couple of days. I am glad Fred doesn't smoke.' 'Yah what?' the bald headed man replied. 'It's all right dear I am not talking to you. I am talking about you, carry on reading the paper,' the lady in the glasses said, as she smiles at her husband, and then returns to her conversation with her friend.

'Then, while she was in Hospital she contracted the MRSA virus; you know that super bug thing that's going around. They say she nearly died from that. She's got this bag thing now for the rest of her life. But she's coping and keeps cheerful, but you don't know what's under the surface do you. I know if it was me, and Fred had been the cause, then his life would be hell, I can tell you.'

'I don't know why I bother buying these papers. The bloody rubbish they put in them is unbelievable. The bloody politically correct get on my tits.' 'Watch your language Fred,' the lady in the glasses said, as she breaks from her conversation with her friend.

'Well, I don't care, it's right isn't it Jim. They are on about banning Christmas now in case they offend non-Christians. Bloody tough that's what I say. What about you Jim?' 'I am keeping out of it, don't drag me into it.' 'What do you mean; it's you who is always going on about this, that and the other. Now you're backing out, what's up with you?'

'Pack it in Fred, if Jim doesn't want to pass comment, leave him alone,' the lady in the glasses said, as she nudges Fred in the ribs.

'What's that for?' Fred protests. 'That's to shut you up.'

'Can't a bloke pass an opinion any more?' 'No, now be quiet,' his wife says, as Fred shakes his newspaper and turns over the page.

His wife carries on talking to her friend. 'You should have heard him Betty on the way to the airport he drove me mad. He was moaning all the way about the driver of this car, and that car. Traffic lights, Islands, Speed Cameras the lot. I told him if he didn't shut up, I was going on holiday on my own.' 'Jim was the same. I don't know what's the matter with them, they are like grumpy old men,' Betty said to her friend.

The two men looked at each other, and Fred winked at Jim and they both started smiling at each other behind their newspapers, and then they started laughing. 'I'll clobber you two in a minute,' the lady in the glasses said. 'It's not me Sheila, it's him.' 'They are like two little kids,' Sheila said to Betty. 'I was thinking of enrolling them into the grumpy old gits club, what do you think?' Sheila said. 'What a good idea,' Betty replied.

It's wonderful to see the colour of life, Stuart thinks to himself, as he looks up at the boarding screen, and sees their flight number has moved up to the half waypoint, but still no time or boarding gate number.

'I am off to the loo,' Claire says to her mom. 'I'll come with you. Look after the bags will you love we won't be long,' Tricia says to Stuart as the girls head for the toilets.

Stuart looks back at the boarding screen and sees they have finally come up with boarding instructions. Flight MAM 275 to Faro, boarding now gate 15. He sees various people get up, and start to make their way to the doors leading to the boarding gates, including the elderly foursome opposite, and Sheila is heard to say, 'Come on Fred it looks like we're off'. Fred folds his newspaper up and picks his hand luggage up and turns to his wife. 'Pity, I was just getting into that article.' 'Well you will have plenty of time on the plane to finish it off, now shift.'

I hope they are not staying in our hotel Stuart thinks to himself, as he sees them make their way to the departure lounge.

'Well it looks like your wait is nearly over they are just calling us to board the plane,' Stuart says to the couple next to him. 'Right, come on Michael,' The lady says to her husband as they both get up, and pick up their bags, and begin to make their way towards gate 15.

'See you later,' the lady says. 'Yes ok,' Stuart replies, as he watches them make their way across the lounge to the corridor leading to the boarding gates. He also sees the lady with her two girls get up and make their way in the same direction. Stuart thinks it seems they are on our flight as well.

Oh God, where are the girls he thinks to himself as he sits there with the bags.

'When your Mom and Claire get back I am going to the toilet are you coming?' Stuart asks Craig. 'Yes ok.'

A few minutes pass by, which seem an age to Stuart as he sits there waiting, and finally he sees Tricia and Claire ambling along towards them.

'They have just started to board the plane, Craig and I are just going to the loo, we won't be a minute,' Stuart says.

Stuart and Craig use the toilet and Craig finishes first, and makes a dash for the door. 'Hey where are you going young man, you haven't washed your hands, now get back here and do as you are told.' Craig stops dead in his tracks, and returns to the hand basins, and runs the tap and washes his hands. He then walks towards the hand drier on the wall, and puts his hands underneath it. It switches on automatically and the warm air blows over his hands. Stuart washes his hands and makes for the next drier.

'Don't get dashing off without me,' he says to Craig. Stuart finishes and they leave, and make their way to the girls.

Chapter 19

'Right, have we got everything?' Stuart asks Tricia, who is standing there holding the flight bag. 'Yes I have the boarding tickets and passports.'

They make their way through the doors and down the long corridor towards boarding gate fifteen. As they arrive, they see other passengers all sitting together waiting to board the plane; they find a seat and sit down to wait for the final call.

Stuart looks at his watch and the time is six twenty five. They are all feeling anxious as the final minutes to boarding tick away.

Suddenly the door leading to the aircraft walkway opens, and two Flight Attendants walk through and stand behind a small desk. One of the Attendants turns to the back of them and picks up a microphone, and addresses the waiting passengers over the tannoy.

'Would all passengers for the MAM two seven five flight to Faro sitting in rows one to ten please come forward to board the plane.'

Craig says 'Is that us Dad?' 'No we will be next.' Stuart watches as the queue passes the Attendant and she tears off part of the boarding tickets, and the various passengers make their way down the long corridor leading to the plane. He sees the last passengers pass through the doorway.

A couple of minute's pass by and the Attendant turns and reaches for the microphone again. 'Would all passengers in rows eleven to twenty please come forward?' 'That's us,' Stuart says, and they get up and make their way towards the gate. He sees the man and lady whose first flight it was are also in the queue, and the lady with the two girls.

They eventually reach the front of the queue. Tricia has the boarding tickets and hands them to the Attendant. The Attendant tears them off and says 'Have a nice holiday.' 'We will,' Tricia says, as they make their way down the corridor towards the plane.

Stuart notices the air in the corridor is getting colder the closer he gets to the plane, and the noise of an engine can be heard quietly in the background. He also starts to smell a faint trace of burnt kerosene in the air.

They reach the doorway of the plane and two more Flight Attendants in their smart blue uniforms greet them.

Tricia shows the tickets to the Attendant who smiles and says. 'You're just on the right, about halfway down with one seat on the left of the isle.' 'Thank you,'

Tricia says, as she makes her way slowly down the isle, with Craig and Claire behind, followed by Stuart.

Tricia is looking at the seat row numbers on the bottom of the overhead lockers, and counts them until she sees row twenty. She stops and allows Craig to get to his seat, followed by Claire and finely herself. Stuart looks at the seat on the opposite side of the isle and sees row twenty seat D. He also sees the couple he had been sat next to in the departure lounge are also sitting on the same row. 'Oh hello, it looks like I am sitting next to you for the flight,' as he sits down next to the lady who smiles back at him as he settles into his seat.

Having placed their flight bags in the overhead locker, Tricia and the children settle down in their seats. Craig has the window seat and Claire is in the middle. Tricia fastens her seat belt and assists Claire with hers.

'Is that tight enough?' She asks Claire. 'Yes it's fine thanks.' 'Help Craig with his will you,' Tricia asks Claire.

'Put your seat belt on?' Claire says to Craig who looks puzzled at the fastening buckle on the lap belt. 'I have but it's too loose.'

Claire gets hold of the buckle and pulls the loose end tight. 'Is that ok?' 'No it's too tight I can't breath.' 'It's tight enough then.'

'Mom she's made it too tight I can't breathe.' 'Oh loosen it off Claire and stop messing about.'

Claire loosens the belt. 'Is that ok I wouldn't want it too loose, you might fall out when we take off,' Claire says to Craig, who is still wriggling about in the seat. 'Mam she says I am going to fall out if it's too loose when we take off.' 'Oh don't be silly, and stop it Claire, you are frightening him.' 'Good we might get some peace.'

Craig reaches forward and looks in the seat pocket of the seat in front to see what's in there. He finds a big card with pictures of an aeroplane floating on the sea and people sliding down a slide into the water.

'What's that for?' he asks Claire. She looks at the card. 'That's what happens when you don't keep still, and stop asking stupid questions. It's obvious isn't it; if the plane crashes on the water you jump out and slide down the chute.'

He continues looking in the seat pocket and finds a brown paper bag.

'What's this for?' he asks Claire. 'Oh for God sake, it's for when you are sick. Now put it back and look out of the window and make sure the wing is still there.'

'What's up with him now?' Tricia asks Claire. 'Oh he is driving me mad with what's this for, what's that for. He wanted to know what the brown bag was for so I told him. I also told him to look out of the window and make sure the wing was still there. I haven't heard any more. So that might keep him quiet for a bit.'

Stuart turns to the lady he met in the lounge whose first flight this is and says 'Let me introduce myself. I am Stuart, and my wife over there is Tricia, and my two kids are Claire and Craig.' 'I am Gill, and this is my husband Michael,' the lady replies. 'I am pleased to meet you both,' Stuart says. 'Where are you from?' he asks. ' We're from a small village just East of Leicester.' 'Oh I went there once, but I am better now,' Stuart says and they laugh at his joked remark.

'Where are you from?' Gill asks. 'Oh we are from Worcestershire,' he says not wishing to inform her with too much detail of where they lived in case he bored her. 'Worcester has a nice Cathedral hasn't it?' Gill says. 'Yes and one or two nice pubs,' Stuart says, as they both laugh.

People continue to pass down the plane, and Stuart looks down the central isle towards the cockpit, and sees various people moving about. He sees a man in a yellow jacket enter the plane, and turn to his left and enter the cockpit. As the door opens he can see the cabin crew inside and all the various instruments. The man in the yellow jacket hands a clipboard to the Pilot in the left-hand seat who looks at it and signs it.

The Captain looks to be aged about 45 years, with fair hair, and slim build, and about five feet eight inches tall, with a fresh and healthy complexion. There is a short conversation between the crew and the man in the yellow jacket and they can be seen to be laughing at the conversation they were all having, and then the man leaves the cockpit and closes the door, and exits the plane.

Stuart is also aware of a Stewardess walking down the isle towards him, closing the overhead lockers on either side. She passes by, and closes lockers as she carries on towards the rear.

Stuart turns to Tricia and says, 'Is every thing ok over there?' 'Yes,' She replies. 'What about Craig?' he asks. 'Yes he's fine.'

Craig looks across at his Dad and waves. Stuart puts his fist to his mouth and makes a chewing action of nerves about the prospect of the forth-coming flight.

The Stewardess now walks forward checking each of the passengers has their seat belts fastened, and checking to make sure there are no heavy bags lying loose on the floor.

Stuart is aware the lady with the two young blonde girls is sitting directly infront of him. He sees her head move to the right as she talks to the two girls, but he can't hear what is said.

He sees the Stewardess walk towards the cabin door on the left. She reaches out and grabs the big heavy door, which seems far too heavy for her to handle, and she pulls it with comparative ease and slams it shut, and puts the handle into the locked position.

'It looks like we're nearly ready for the off,' Stuart says to Gill. Gill does not offer a reply, but smiles in an apprehensive way, and looks out of the window.

The tannoy is heard to click on 'Good morning everyone,' a male voice was heard to say over the chitter chatter of the passengers. There was a pause and the passenger noise died down. 'This is Captain Martin Gibson welcoming you to Air Five Thousands flight to Faro, myself and my First Officer John Cutler hope you have a good flight with us this morning. The weather in Faro is currently in the mid twenties with clear blue skies. We shall be flying down over the south of England, across the English Channel, across the Bay of Biscay into Northern Spain, then Portugal before turning into Faro. Your Flight Attendants today are Senior Attendant Zoe, with Emma and Chris at the back. Hopefully they will be serving a hot meal in a short while. Our journey time should be about two hours and forty-five minutes. Enjoy the flight, and I will speak to you again after your meal.' The tannoy clicks off.

'I've entered the flight plan into the main computer and it all checks ok,' John says to Martin the Captain, who is sitting in the left-hand seat. John continues to read the flight checklist to Martin, who listens intently as the various items are read and double-checked by him.

'We have one hundred and fifty passengers, ten tons of fuel, with seven point five tons in the burn. Parking Brake off. (Martin reaches down by his side and releases the parking brake.) Pitot heat on, and John reaches up to the overhead panel and switches the Pitot heater on. Collision lights on. (He reaches up to the overhead panel and switches them on.) Autopilot on. (He switches the autopilot to the on position.) Avionics on, Flight director on, Auto throttle armed, Transponder on.' As John has named the various items he has switched on, Martin has watched him carry out the operations.

John continues his conversation with Martin. ' It is expected we shall be using runway three three today, with a right turn out onto track for Honiley and the Brecon beacon. Our diversion air field will be East Midlands, and that will also be a right turn out after take off.' 'That's fine, are we ready to push back and start now?' Martin asks John. 'Yes I am ready when you are. Do you want me to fly down today?' John asks. 'Yes if you like,' Martin replies.

Martin puts his headset on, and switches the microphone over to talk to the ground staff. 'This is the Captain speaking, how are things down there?' 'We're okay and ready when you are. The tunnel has been pulled clear of the aircraft. Chokes have been removed, and the Tractor is coupled up,' the Ground Engineer says to Martin. 'Okay I'll ask the Tower for clearance to push back and start.'

Martin switches the microphone over to the radio set, and at the same time sets the radio frequency to one two one, eight zero for the Ground Controller. 'Hawk two seven five requesting push back and start.' 'Push back and start approved,' the Ground Controller replied from the Control Tower.

Martin switches over his microphone to talk to the ground staff. 'Push back and start clearance given, ready when you are sunshine.' 'Okay here we go then.'

The Ground Engineer signals to the tractor driver to start to push the aircraft backwards away from the dock. The tractors engine is heard by the Engineer to rise in revs, and the aircraft very slowly starts to move backwards. The Engineer walks with the aircraft still coupled to it by his long head set wire.

'It looks like we are moving,' Stuart says to Gill next to him, as he looks out of the window and sees the scenery slowly pass by. It is a strange feeling, it is as if they are stationary and everything else is moving. Stuart looks across at Craig, who looks back at him across the isle and smiles. Stuart puts his thumb up as if to say yes we're off, but he can't make himself heard due to the distance they are apart.

The plane slowly turns to its right onto the taxiway and eventually stops. 'You can start the engines when you are ready,' the Ground Engineer says to Martin. 'Yes okay, starting now.'

Martin reaches down to the centre console by the throttle levers and puts the number one and two engine idle switches to the run position. He then reaches up to the overhead panel and turns the number one engine starter switch on, and turns it clockwise to the start position, and holds it in that position, and the engine starts to turn. A faint whining noise is heard which gets louder and louder, and suddenly the engine burst into life. He releases the starter switch as he sees the engine percentage power gauge rise and fall, and eventually settle at twenty three percent of N1 power, and the switch returns to its generator position in order to give the aircraft it's electrical power.

He repeats the process for the number two-engine starter switch next to number one, and the starboard engine burst into life. Again he watches the N1gauge settle to twenty three percent of power. A check is also made of the readings given by the EGT (Exhaust Gas Temperature) gauges, which are reading normal. Having placed the parking brake back on he lets the engines warm up a short while.

'Is everything alright down there?' Martin asks the Ground Engineer. 'Yes everything is okay here, have a good flight. See you when you get back.' 'Thanks,' Martin replies, as the Engineer disconnects his microphone cable from the aircraft and closes the flap. Martin watches out of the port window, and sees the Engineer walk away from the aircraft, and the tractor with its yellow flashing light drives off to get ready to start the push back on another aircraft.

'Hawk two seven five requesting Taxiway,' Martin asks the Ground Controller in the Control Tower. 'Taxiway echo one, for runway three three, QNH one zero one four, right and left at the end of the taxiway then hold, and contact tower on one one eight decimal three zero, squawk two three two five.' Martin reads back the instructions given. 'Read back correct,' the Ground Controller says.

Martin releases the parking brake, and John slowly pushes the throttle levers forward to increase the engine power, and the aircraft slowly moves forward. He steers the aircraft with the control column just like a car, and follows the yellow lines leading to runway three three take off area.

As the aircraft slowly makes it's way towards the runway, Senior Flight Attendant Zoe picks up the tannoy microphone to speak to the passengers, as Emma stands in the centre of the isle at the front, and Chris stands in the isle at the middle of the aircraft.

'In order to ensure your safety in the event of an emergency, I must point out to you the emergency exits. There are two at the front of the aircraft, two in the middle over each wing, and two at the back. In the event of an emergency, exit the aircraft via your nearest door. Under your seat you will find a life jacket, place this over your head, cross the tie straps round the back and tie at the front. To inflate the jacket pull the cord down sharply. Do not inflate until you have exited the aircraft. Re-inflation can be given by blowing into the tube. There is a whistle to attract attention. All shoes with high heels must be removed before exiting the plane. Chutes will be deployed, and should there be a loss of air pressure, oxygen masks will fall automatically. Pull the elastic back and place over your head, and put the mask over your face and breathe normally.'

While Zoe was speaking, the other two Flight Attendants were demonstrating with their hands the exit doors and the operation of the life jacket. 'We hope you have a good flight, and we shall be providing drinks from the drinks trolley shortly after take off.'

Zoe switches the microphone off. The tannoy is heard to come on again.

'Flight Attendants to take off seats,' Martin said to the Flight Attendants as the aircraft continued towards the runway.

106

Chapter 20

John reaches the holding point and stops the aircraft as requested.

'Hawk two seven five at holding point requesting take off clearance,' Martin asks the tower over the radio. 'Hawk two seven five hold, I have one coming in 4 miles, you will be cleared after it clears the runway.' 'Holding,' Martin replies.

John sets the flaps to five degrees for take off. 'Flaps set five degrees,' John says to Martin who is looking to his left out of the port window and sees an approaching aircraft with its landing lights on. It gets closer and closer and passes infront of them, floating down and down until it touches the tarmac runway, and blue smoke from its tyres can be seen to rise in the air and swirl round until it dissipates completely.

They both wait and watch the aircraft clear the runway. 'Hawk two seven five line up three three, contact radar one one eight zero five, and you are cleared for take off,' the Tower Controller told Martin. Martin reads the message back.

John moves the throttles forward, and the aircraft moves very slowly forward and turns right, and lines up with the centre line of runway three three. John sets the heading bug to three three one degrees, in order to keep the aircraft flying in a straight line down the runway and after take off. This not only reduces his work load, but ensures the aircraft will fly in a straight line after take off, until they are required to make their right turn to clear the residential area below.

John puts his left hand onto both throttle levers. Martin places his hands over them covering John's, as a safety precaution should anything happen, which might cause John to abort the take off in an emergency. 'Ready,' John says. 'Lets go then,' Martin replies, as John pushes the throttle levers forward to full power, and the percent power gauges rise towards one hundred percent of N1, and the engines power starts to accelerate the aircraft down the runway.

The plane gathers speed pushing the passengers back into their seats, and the noise from the engines rise to a thunderous roar, and the plane is soon travelling faster than a formula one racing car.

The aircraft bumps along the runway. John watches the indicated air speed indicator dial as the aircraft passes eighty knots. At this point the aircraft could be stopped before it reached the end of the runway, should the need arise.

The aircraft passes one hundred knots. The tension between the two Pilot's rise, and their hearts beat faster as the adrenaline surges into their body. They reach one hundred and forty knots 'Vee one,' John shouts out.

At this speed, the aircraft would not be able to stop before the end of the runway, should there be a problem.

A split second later the aircraft's speed has reached over one hundred and forty three knots or over two hundred miles per hour, and at this speed the aircraft will lift off the runway.

'Vee R Rotate,' John shouts, and at the same time eases the control column back. The aircraft's nose starts to lift up, as the power from the engines pushes the aircraft into the air, and the bumping stops, and a relative peace now exists within. The aircraft is airborne at five minutes past seven.

The speed rises, and also the altitude meter starts to rise, and the dial rotates infront of John in a clockwise direction, the numbers in the centre of the dial start to increase as the plane passes five hundred feet, climbing at the rate of eighteen hundred feet per minute.

They are now travelling in excess of one hundred and fifty knots with a positive rate of climb. 'Gear up,' John says, as Martin reaches down and moves the gear up lever upwards to raise the under carriage. The wheels are heard to swing up into the body of the aircraft, the doors are heard to close, as the under carriage down lights on the console go out.

John sets the speed of the aircraft to two hundred and fifty knots. The speed at which the aircraft is not to exceed below ten thousand feet.

They maintain their straight-ahead bearing of three three one degrees and are still climbing. They pass eight hundred feet, nine hundred feet, one thousand feet. 'Flaps back to one,' John says, as he moves the flap lever forward to the first setting.

The aircraft continues to accelerate to two hundred knots and still climbing as they reach one thousand five hundred feet, as John sets the flaps to zero.

Martin switches his microphone on to talk to Birmingham Radar Controller. 'Hawk two seven five passing two thousand feet.' 'Turn right onto a heading of one seven zero and contact London on one three three seven zero good-bye,' the Radar Controller said as Martin reads back the instructions.

John switches on the GPS (Ground Positioning Satellite System), and then presses the Navigational Directional button. This puts the aircraft into the control of the autopilot, and turns the aircraft slowly to the right onto the flight plan track for the Honiley Radio beacon situated south west of Birmingham.

The Non-Directional Radio Beacons (NDB) allows an aircraft to fly in a controlled pattern between places, and not to aimlessly fly around the sky.

Stuart looks out of the starboard side window to his right and sees the ground, which looks very picturesque in the early morning mist.

Martin changes the frequency on his number one set to one three three seven zero and calls the London Air Traffic Controller. 'Hawk two seven five heading one seven zero for Honiley.' 'Hawk two seven five turn right onto heading two three eight. You are cleared to flight level one nine zero, report on reaching to London one three two eight zero good-bye,' the Controller says, as Martin reads back the instructions.

The aircraft continues on its journey as the speed increases to two hundred and fifty knots, and it climbs towards ten thousand feet. John reduces the flaps back to zero, and switches the seat belt on lights for the passengers to the off position.

Normality returns to the passengers as they relax from the stress of the take off, and unbuckle their seat belts. The Flight Attendants release their seat belts and start to prepare the light refreshments trolleys in the galley area for the passengers.

'That wasn't too bad was it love?' Michael says to Gill. 'I have had better experiences,' she says.

Stuart looks across to Tricia and the kids 'Okay love,' he says to Tricia. 'Yes I am fine.' She turns to her left and says to Craig, 'Are you ok,' he nods his head in reply. 'Is the wing still there?' Claire asks him. 'Yes of course it is, don't be stupid,' he snaps back.

Stuart reaches forward and lowers the table in the back of the seat infront of him in readiness for the drinks, and hopefully later for breakfast.

The aircraft has small TV sets, set into the ceiling of the plane and adverts are being shown. Craig's attention is drawn to the TV as he watches the adverts go off and cartoons begin.

Zoe helps Emma get her trolley ready. 'Is every thing there?' she asks Emma. 'No I want some Ice cubes, could you pass some please?' she asks. Zoe turns round to the fridge and opens the door and reaches in to get a pre packed bag of Ice cubes which she passes back to Emma, who places them into a small ice bucket on top of her trolley. 'Okay off you go, I'll get started on the breakfasts,' Zoe says, as Emma makes her way down the isle with her trolley and stops at the first passengers.

'What would you like to drink?' Michael asks Gill. 'Oh just a fruit juice.' 'I think I'll have a scotch with ice,' he adds.

Stuart turns to Tricia. 'When the drinks trolley gets here order what you want for you and the kids and I'll pay ok.'

Tricia turns to Claire. 'What do you want off the drinks trolley?' 'I'll have an orange juice please,' she replies. 'Craig what do you want?' 'Orange,' he says. 'What else?' and looks angrily waiting for the key word. 'Please,' came the reply. 'Thank you,' she says.

Emma slowly works her way backwards down the isle, until she reaches row twenty where Tricia and Stuart are seated. She turns to her left and speaks to Tricia.

'What drinks would you like?' she asks. 'Three orange juices please.' Emma reaches into the cupboard infront of her and gets three cans of orange juice out and shakes them, and opens them, and pours them into three small plastic glasses all with white antidrip mats on the bases.

'Would you like ice in them?' she asks. 'Please,' Tricia replies, and Emma uses a small scoop to shovel ice cubes from the ice bucket into the glasses. She passes them over one by one. 'Thank you,' Tricia says. 'My Husband over there will pay,' she adds. 'The soft drinks are free.' 'Oh brilliant thanks,' Tricia says, as Emma turns to Stuart.

'What would you like Sir?' Emma asks. 'Could I have a coke please with ice?' Emma opens a can of coke and pours it into a plastic glass and hands it to Stuart.

Michael leans forward and says to Emma. 'I'll have a scotch with ice, and a pineapple juice for my wife please.'

Emma reaches into her cupboard and selects three small bottles of scotch whiskey and shows them to Michael. 'Which would you like?' she asks. 'I'll have the Glenfiddich please.' Emma puts two ice cubes into the glass and passes the bottle of whiskey and glass over to Michael. She then opens a small can of pineapple juice for Gill, and pours it into the glass along with the ice and passes it to her.

'That will be one pound fifty for the whiskey,' Emma says to Michael, who hands her a five-pound note. Emma counts the change and passes it back. Emma releases the foot brake on her trolley and continues backwards down the isle to the next row of passengers.

After ten minutes of flying time, Hawk two seven five is on track for the Brecon beacon in Wales, with sixty-one miles to go and now at a height of flight level (FL) 130 (13,000 feet) the speed is increased to three hundred knots. Martin has already set the radio frequency for the next London Air Traffic Controller to one three two eight zero.

'Hawk to seven five London flight level one nine zero,' Martin says to the London ATC.

'Hawk two seven five climb to flight level two five zero and report level to London on one three four four five good bye,' the London Controller told Martin who reads back the transmission. John changes the altitude meter on the centre console to twenty five thousand feet, and the aircraft starts to climb. The auto throttles increase the speed to compensate for the drag, as the aircraft starts its climb. John looks round the various dials and gauges to ensure all is well.

'It makes a change to be approaching Wales in fine weather,' Martin says to John. 'Yes we have a good high pressure over us and all the way down.'

Claire finishes her fruit juice drink, and reaches under her table, and pulls out the in-flight shopping magazine from the seat pocket infront of her, and begins to look through the pages of duty free shopping.

Craig is still watching the TV intensely, and the cartoons have finished, and a Mr Bean film is showing. Mr Bean is going on holiday and is packing his clothes into a very small suitcase. This requires various items being cut to fit the small case. The actions of Mr Bean amuse Craig, which distracts him from the aspects of the flight. A young boy much like Craig, who is sitting next to Mr Bean and unbeknown to him, has been sick in the brown paper bag. Mr Bean decides to take the bag off the boy and blow it up, and bang the bag in order to make the distressed boy laugh. Craig burst out laughing, and so does everyone else on the plane including Stuart. 'That bit slays me,' Stuart says to Gill sitting next to him. She is not amused, and infact it makes her feel sick to watch it. 'Excuse me please,' she says to Stuart. 'I shall have to go to the loo.' Stuart gets up from his seat, and Gill makes for the front of the plane to the toilet near to the flight deck door.

'Was it something I said,' Stuart says to Michael, who is by now laughing so much he almost chokes on his whiskey.

Fifteen minutes after take off Hawk two seven five is thirty-five miles from the Brecon beacon in Wales, and has levelled off at flight level (FL) two five zero (25,000Feet). Martin reports the aircraft's height to the London ATC on one three four four five and his transmission is cleared. John looks at the flight plan on the computer screen infront of him, and sees the aircraft will turn left onto a heading of one nine two degrees from Brecon towards the beacons at Numpo, Exmoor, and Berryhead.

As they approach the Brecon beacon Martin calls London Air Traffic Controller (ATC) 'Hawk two seven five, five miles from Brecon.' 'Hawk two seven five turn left onto heading one nine two for Berryhead.' Martin replies, 'Hawk two seven five heading one nine two.' 'You are cleared now to flight level three two zero report Berryhead to London on one three three six zero.' 'Cleared flight level three two zero report Berryhead to London on one three three six zero,' Martin replies.

Because the plane is on its flight-planned route, programmed into its computers, and with less than two miles to go to the Brecon beacon, the plane will turn automatically to its left as it reaches the beacon.

Both John and Martin watch the distance measuring equipment (DME) on the computer screen change the nautical miles down in numbers quite quickly as they get closer to the beacon.

As they reach the beacon, the plane banks to its left and eventually levels off onto a heading of one nine two degrees south and the (DME) reading shows the distance to the Numpo beacon of seven nautical miles. John changes the altitude meter to 32,000 feet for FL320. Hawk two seven five starts its climb to flight level three two zero as they head for the south coast of England.

They have eighty miles to go before they reach the beacon at Berryhead and the English coast, and they will need all this distance to reach flight level three two zero.

Gill returns to her seat. 'Okay now?' Michael enquires as she settles back in her seat. 'Yes I wasn't sick, but I felt like it,' she replies.

'I am sorry if I upset you,' Stuart remarks to Gill. 'It wasn't your fault, it was a combination of the flight, plus what I saw on the TV that did it,' she said. 'Any way I never introduced myself to you properly, I am a Schoolteacher by trade, and what do you two do for your sins?' he asks them. Gill replies 'I own my own Greengrocery Business and Michael is a Transport Manager for a large Construction Company.' 'Very nice. That's something I have always wanted to do is work for myself, and may be one day you never know,' Stuart replies.

Emma has now begun to collect all the glasses from the drinks round, while Zoe starts to load up the trolleys with the breakfasts for everyone, which have been heated in the special aircraft ovens.

'You will love the in-flight meals, they have been made into a fine art form,' Stuart says to Gill making the conversation carry on between them.

'They have to be appetising to the public, and compact and light in weight. You certainly won't put on weight with the amounts the air operators provide, but they are wholesome, and quite filling in their way,' he adds. 'I look forward to it, I am starving,' she remarks. They both smell the air and take in the fumes of cooked bacon and bake beans as it drifts down the plane towards them.

The in-flight work carried out by the Flight Attendants is very hectic, as they have less than three hours to deal with everything before they reach their destination.

Chapter 21

With the early morning sunshine lighting up the sky, Craig was able to look out of his window and see the pretty patterns of the fields below, and the roads and rivers as the plane increased its height.

John monitors the engine's instruments, and sees they are running at ninety seven percent of N1, as it climbs towards thirty two thousand feet, climbing at a rate of six hundred feet per minute.

It's been thirty-seven minutes since they left Birmingham as they approach the south coast of England. Craig is looking out of his window and sees the sea. He turns to his mother in an excited manner and remarks to her. 'I can see the sea Mom,' he says and turns back to the window pointing down to it for his mother to see. Tricia can just make out the coast from her isle seat. 'Oh yes I see it,' she replies.

'Hawk two seven five approaching Berryhead,' Martin says to the London ATC. 'Hawk two seven five, turn left onto heading one eight seven, you are cleared to Salco, report to Brest on one three four eight two, Good Bye,' the ATC controller says, as Martin repeats the transmission.

Martin re-sets the radio frequency to the Brest ATC on one three four eight two. Hawk two seven five reaches the Berryhead beacon, and turns automatically onto a compass heading of one eight seven degrees, and they start to cross the English channel leaving England behind, as they head for France. They have now reached flight level FL 320.

'Get your table down,' Claire says to Craig, 'Breakfast's on its way.' Craig reaches forward and unfolds his table tray from the back of the seat infront.

Emma is making her way backwards down the isle, handing the breakfasts out as she goes. She reaches row twenty, and passes a breakfast tray across to Craig, and then Claire, and finally Tricia, before she passes them across to Stuart, Gill, and Michael.

Craig looks at his breakfast, and is amazed at the contents of the tray. He sees he has a cup, and inside is a small carton of butter, and one of marmalade, and a carton of milk. There is a white bun in a clear plastic bag, a small tub of orange juice, and a large container sealed up with what he assumes is his cooked breakfast inside.

There is also a clear plastic bag, with a knife, fork and spoon, and two little packets of salt and pepper, a tube of red sauce and one of brown, and a sachet of sugar. There's a sachet of freshener to wipe your hands on after breakfast.

He tries to peel the foil from the top of the container, but it's too hot for him. 'It's hot,' he says to Claire as the foil lid burnt his fingers slightly as he tried to peel the lid off. Claire reaches over and grabs the corner of the foil lid and peels it back. 'Thanks,' he says, as he looks at the contents and sees two small sausages, some scrabbled egg; bake beans, and a small hash brown.

He doesn't know where to start first. He watches Claire open the bun first. Then the bag with all the knives and forks in, and takes the knife out and cuts the bun open. She then reaches into the cup, and gets the butter out, and spreads it onto the bun. She continues to get the tomato sauce out of the bag and opens it, and pours it over her breakfast.

Having seen Claire making her start on her breakfast, he does the same, but the plastic bag with the knife and fork in is a bit tough for him to open. He pulls it as hard as he can, and suddenly it rips open, and spills its contents all over the tray. 'Oh God, what have you done now?' Claire says, looking at the mess her little brother has made.

'I couldn't help it, it wouldn't open,' he says. 'Never mind,' Tricia says, as Claire helps her brother pick up the various items. 'Now try not to make another mess,' she says as she starts to tuck into her breakfast.

Zoe the Senior Flight attendant is an attractive petite brunette in her early thirties, and has been with the airline for five years on the European routes. Despite her responsibilities, she has a good sense of humour, and needs one, having to deal with people from all walks of life, as well as fellow crewmembers.

She opens the cockpit cabin door, and the noise level within the cabin is quite high compared to the rest of the plane. She steps inside, and closes the door behind her, and looks out of the front window, and sees blue sky and sunshine. 'Now boys, what delicious delights can I tempt you two with this morning?' she asks Martin and John. 'Oh what's on offer. Caviar and chips again I suppose?' Martin replies.

'No you cheeky chap, it's either the exciting breakfast, or the chicken dinner. You can please yourselves, because on the return flight it will be the same, and you know the rules, you can't have the same meal anyway.' Martin asks John, 'Which do you prefer?' 'No, you are the Captain you should have the first choice.' 'God he's nice isn't he. Well let me see. I will have the Breakfast.' 'Right Ok,' Zoe says, as she exits the cabin.

She enters the galley and places their order into the oven to heat for a few minutes.

Martin calls Brest ATC on one three four eight two, 'Hawk two seven five cleared Salco mid channel, on heading one eight seven. Flight level three two zero.' 'Maintain, report crossing coast,' the ATC controller said in English, but with a French accent, as all Aircraft transmissions are in English.

After a few minutes, Zoe opens the oven door, and removes the two meals for Martin and John, and places one on top of the other, and re enters the cockpit cabin. 'Now then this is yours,' she hands Martin his breakfast tray, and then passes the chicken dinner over to John.

'How are things doing back there?' Martin asks. 'Not too bad. A bit busy, they have just been given their breakfasts. I'll be back in a bit with some coffee Ok,' Zoe says, as she makes for the door. 'Brill, thanks,' Martin says, as he starts to eat his breakfast.

'They're not bad these meals you know. What's yours like?' Martin asks John. 'Yes it's ok, I have had better,' he replies. 'I've got two days off after this flight,' Martin says to John. 'My wife and I are off to Hampshire to visit friends for a couple of days.'

'I've got a flight to Salzburg and Dusseldorf,' John replies. 'The Salzburg flight is a good one. I did that a few weeks ago along with Innsbruck. That's got a ten thousand feet approach height, quite scary in the dark.' 'I imagine it is,' John replies.

'That was good,' Martin says, as he finishes off his breakfast. 'Where's that wench with the coffee,' he says. 'You had better not say that to her face, she might smack you one.' They both snigger. 'She's a good lass, got three kids you know, you wouldn't believe it. Ask her if you don't believe me,' Martin says to John, who has just finished his meal, as the cabin door opens, and in steps Zoe.

'It's right isn't it, you have three kids?' Martin asks Zoe. 'Yes, two girls and a boy,' She replies. 'Non of them are mine,' Martin says and they all laugh. 'Come on, stop messing about, and give me that cup if you don't want the coffee poured all over you,' Zoe says to Martin. Martin turns round towards Zoe holding his cup as she pours in the coffee. 'What are their names?' Martin asks. 'Beth, and Laura, she's four next month, and baby James who is almost one now.' 'Good for you gal,' Martin says, as Zoe pours John's coffee into his cup. 'Are you taking the duty free orders for us for the return flight?' Martin asks Zoe. 'Yes if you like. What do you want?'

'A bottle of Whiskey, bottle of Vodka and a small Gin. What do you want?' Martin asks John, 'Nothing for me.' 'Oh come on, you have to give an order. If you don't want it I'll buy it off you when we get back.' 'Ok, just a whiskey and brandy then please.' 'Ok that's two whiskeys, vodka, gin and a brandy, I'll sort it.' 'Thanks,' Martin says, as Zoe leaves the cabin.

'She's a good kid,' Martin says to John. 'We are approaching the French coast,' John says to Martin. 'Oh yes, I had better let Brest know where we are,' he says, as he switches the radio transmitter on. 'Hawk two seven five approaching the coast.' 'Maintain to Quimper and report on reaching,' the Brest . ATC Controller says, as Martin repeats the transmission.

They cross the French coast between Côte Du Leon and Côte De Granit Rose, south west of Jersey, and heading for the beacon at Quimper. Quimper is a reasonable size town, situated just in land from the Côte De Cornouaille, with its beautiful beaches mid way between Lorient and Brest itself. It boasts of a beautiful Cathedral and some of the nicest Café's and Restaurants, and Arts and Craft Centres in the region, and very much a popular tourist area.

They have been flying now for an hour since they left Birmingham. Emma is dispensing the coffee or tea to the passengers. She reaches row twenty. 'Tea or Coffee?' she asks Tricia. 'Tea please,' and at the same time both Claire and Craig also ask for tea and hand their cups to Emma, where they place them on the tray she has offered to them. Emma pours the tea into the cups and hands the tray back, and they remove their cups.

Seven minutes after crossing the French coast they reach Quimper. Martin calls Brest ATC, 'Hawk two seven five approaching Quimper.' 'Turn right onto two zero five and maintain,' the ATC Controller informs Martin, who reads back the transmission.

The plane turns right eighteen degrees, onto a heading of two zero five, and starts to cross the coast of Côte De Cornouaille. The sun worshippers on the beaches below may be looking up in the sky and seeing two vapour trails being made by flight MAM two seven five as it heads south for Northern Spain, across the Bay of Biscay on its way to Faro.

'Do you still play Badminton?' Martin asks John. 'Yes, my wife and I had a couple of games last night down the club. I reckon I didn't do my back any good either. Do you still play Squash?' John asks. 'Yes, but I am not as fit as I ought to be. It really takes it out of me these days. I reckon I ought to take up Badminton instead.' 'Well if you want to join us sometime feel free, and give us a ring, I'd love to take you on.' 'You're on. I am not such a pushover as you might think,' Martin replies. 'We'll see,' John says.

Zoe re-enters the cabin. 'Have you two finished your coffee?' 'Yes my dear we have. I must go to the loo. Are you ok for a minute?' Martin asks John. 'Yes I am fine.' Martin struggles out of his seat and leaves the cabin, and makes for the toilet just outside.

Someone is using the toilet, so Martin has to wait, and there is also a small queue as well. The first person in the line is a middle-aged lady.

'Now I hate to have to pull rank on you,' Martin says, 'my needs are greater than yours, and I am the Captain.' They both laugh. 'I shan't be a minute, I promise. Only I have left the Flight Attendant in charge, and God knows what she might do.' They both laugh again, as the door opens and a young man exits the toilet. Martin rushes in and closes the door.

A minute later Martin flushes the loo and washes his hands, and opens the door. 'Thanks,' he says to the lady passenger. 'I had better go and see if we are still heading for Faro, or you might not be going on Holiday.' 'We better had,' the lady says, 'Or you will be in trouble.' They both laugh as Martin holds the door for the lady to enter the toilet. He returns to the cabin, and finds Zoe sat in the jump seat behind his seat, talking to John.

Chapter 22

'Is everything Ok?' Martin asks John. 'Yes,' he replies, as Martin struggles to get back into his seat. 'Where are we?' he asks. 'Just passing the West Coast of Bordeaux over to our left,' John replies.

'Ah that's a nice place to go to for your Holiday,' Martin says. 'Did you know, and not many people do, it was built by the Romans in the third Century AD. Did you know that?' he asks Zoe and John.

'No,' they replied. 'It boasts of some of the finest wines in the world, with wines like St Julien, Morec, and Haut Morec, and Pauillac, to name but a few. They produce seven hundred and fifty million bottles of wine a year. I haven't tasted them all I must admit, but the ones I have tasted are very nice indeed.'

'Well I never did,' Zoe remarks. 'Oh yes, he's a bit of a clever Dick is our Martin,' John says and they all laugh. 'Well I can't sit here chatting to you two all day, I had better go and see what's happening out back,' Zoe says, as she leaves the cabin.

She reaches the galley to find Emma disposing of all the breakfast trays and items into the waste container.

'I'll give you a hand,' Zoe says, as she starts to help. Chris bustles into the galley. 'Are there any Breakfasts left for us?' she asks. 'Yes, I think so,' Zoe says. 'Put them in the oven will you, and we can take our break after we have sorted this lot out,' Zoe adds.

Chris places their breakfasts into the oven, as Zoe and Emma finish off disposing of the passenger's breakfasts.

'Ding, Dong' call for an Attendant is heard as a passenger presses the call button for attention. 'If it's that young kid at the back again, I swear I'll kill him,' Chris says, as she storms out of the galley, and makes her way down the plane.

'She doesn't half get upset,' Emma says to Zoe 'I reckon she will blow one of these days, mark my words.' 'She'd better not do it on my shift,' Zoe replies as she continues tidying up the galley.

As they reach the beacon at Lottee, the ATC Controller at Brest speaks to Hawk two seven five. 'Hawk two seven five contact Madrid on one three two five five, goodbye.' Martin repeats the transmission back to Brest ATC. At the same time changes the radio frequency to Madrid ATC. 'Hawk two seven five flight level three two zero heading two zero five.' 'Maintain,' the reply came from the Madrid ATC Controller.

They are now approaching the Northern coast of Spain, and John speaks to the passengers. The aircraft's tannoy is heard to switch on.

'We have just crossed the Bay of Biscay, and we will shortly be passing over the North coast of Spain via Costa Verde in the Asturias region, which has a lovely coastline, with Eucalyptus trees, and beautiful fishing villages. We hope you enjoyed your breakfast, and would passenger Stuart Osborn come to the Flight Deck.' John switches the Intercom off.

'I've asked for that chap I was telling you about to come to the Flight Deck, the one who helped me on the way to the airport when I ran out of Petrol,' John says to Martin. 'Oh yes, that's fine. I look forward to meeting him, and to tell him what a plonker you are.'

'Thanks,' John says. 'Don't mention it,' Martin replies.

Stuart hears his name mentioned on the tannoy, and says to Gill 'Do excuse me, I have been summoned onto the Flight Deck.'

'What's all that about,' she asks. 'I'll tell you all about it when I get back,' he says, as he gets up from his seat.

'I am just going to the Flight Deck,' Stuart says to Tricia. 'We are just going to the loo as well,' she says, as they get up from their seats, and make their way forward towards the toilet and the Flight Deck.

Stuart reaches the cabin door with Craig just behind him. He knocks on the door and opens it. John and Martin look round and smile and John says, 'Come on in.' Stuart starts to enter the cabin. 'Can my young son Craig have a look as well?' he asks.

'Yes of course, come on Craig,' John says. They step inside, and Stuart closes the door behind him. John introduces Stuart to Martin. 'Martin this is Stuart Osborn.' 'Pleased to meet you,' and they shake hands. 'A bit of a plonker wasn't he for running out of petrol,' Martin says. 'You could say that,' Stuart replies.

Craig is bewildered by everything he sees. 'What do you think of all this,' John says to Craig. 'It's brill,' he replies, as he looks at all the dials and screens infront of him. The view from the cockpit of the plane is different, and as he looks out of the window he sees another plane approaching them, but well below them at a terrific speed, as it flashes by on the left side of the plane.

'Do sit down,' John says, pointing to the jump seat just behind Martin.

120

By now Craig has felt comfortable with his new surroundings.

'How fast are we going?' he asks John. 'We are travelling at about five miles a minute, and just over three hundred miles per hour,' John says. 'Gosh,' Craig replies. 'It's just a bit faster than your Dads car,' John adds.

Martin explains quickly some of the functions of the plane, and shows Stuart on the flight plan display screen where they are, and the fact they are about to turn right at the beacon at Aviles onto a heading of two one two degrees. They watch the screen as the plane gets closer, and suddenly as it reaches the beacon, the plane turns right onto the heading for the next beacon at Koret.

'It's as simple as that,' Martin tells Stuart.

'It might be simple to you, but it seems awfully complicated to me,' Stuart replies.

The small talk continues between them for sometime on the technicalities of flying. Craig is bored now. 'Can I go back to Mom?' he asks his dad.

'Yes, and say thank you for letting you see the Flight Deck,' Stuart tells Craig. 'Thank you,' he says. 'Bye,' John says, 'Have a nice Holiday.' 'I will,' Craig says, as he opens the door and exits the cabin, and makes his way back to his seat.

They have been flying now for two hours and twenty-five minutes, when the Air Traffic Controller at Madrid calls Hawk two seven five. 'Hawk two seven five, maintain and contact Lisbon on one two five five five, goodbye.' Martin says, 'Excuse me a minute,' to Stuart as he answers the radio, and repeats the transmission back to Madrid, ensuring he has received their call.

John changes the radio frequency to Lisbon, and Martin checks in with them.

'Hawk two seven five, maintain and report when approaching Viseu,' Martin acknowledges the transmission.

'Everything seems ok now for a bit,' John says to Martin, 'I am just off to the loo. I won't be a minute,' John adds, as he struggles to get out of his seat.

Craig reaches his mom and slides across into his seat. 'Well did you enjoy that?' his mother asks. 'It was brill, and I saw another plane pass us, and it went whiz ever so fast down this side.'

'What's your Dad doing?' Tricia asks. 'He's talking to the man in the Cockpit.' 'I bet he'll be ages, you know what he's like, once he gets started you can't stop him,' she adds.

Emma has started to give out coffee for those people who would like some, and Chris is walking in the opposite direction along the isle with the duty free trolley for the passengers, as John exits the loo and goes to the galley to Zoe.

'Any chance of a coke,' he asks. 'Yes, help yourself, there's some in the fridge back there'.

John reaches down to open the fridge door. 'Arrrrrrrr,' he screams at the top of his voice, and it can be heard right through the plane, as he collapses in a heap onto the galley floor. Zoe spins round and sees John has collapsed.

'What on earth's the matter,' she says, as she bends down to him.

In a strangled faint voice he says, 'It's my back. I can't move. I think I've slipped a disc.'

Zoe gets up and leaves the galley, and enters the main cabin area, and reaches up to one of the overhead lockers, and pulls out a pillow. As she does, Emma approaches.

'What's the matter?' she asks. 'It's John, he's slipped a disc in his back, and he can't move.' 'Oh my God,' Emma replies, as Zoe dashes back to the galley.

'Let me lift your head up and put this pillow under it,' she says, as she gently lifts his head, and slides the pillow under to make him more comfortable. 'How's that feel?' she asks. 'It's ok.'

'I'll just go and tell Martin what's happened,' she says to John.

Emma enters the galley. 'Stay with him a minute while I just tell Martin what's happened.'

Zoe enters the cockpit cabin. 'Sorry to interrupt, but we have a slight problem out there,' she says to Martin who stops talking to Stuart.

'It's John, he's slipped a disc in his back and he can't move.' 'Oh I see. Have you got the situation under control?' Martin says.

'Yes,' Zoe replies. 'Ok, I'll let Lisbon know what's happened.' Zoe leaves the cabin and returns to the galley.

'Hawk two seven five,' Martin says, as he calls Lisbon on the radio. 'Hawk two seven five,' came the reply. 'We have a medical emergency on board. My Co Pilot has slipped a disc in his back, and has collapsed on the floor, and is incapacitated.' 'What do you want to do about it. Do you wish to divert to

Lisbon?' 'No, I would rather carry on to Faro, but if you could inform them of the situation, I would be most grateful,' he says. 'Will do,' the controller replied.

'Well, it's never a dull moment when you're flying, but I never expected this,' Martin says to Stuart. 'I think I ought to go back to my seat,' Stuart says.

'No, just hold tight for a few seconds, and listen out on the radio, and let me know if Lisbon calls back, will you, but don't touch anything?' 'Yes ok,' Stuart replies, as Martin struggles to get out of his seat, and makes his way to the galley.

Martin sees John lying on the floor. 'Now you daft bugger, what have you gone and done?' Martin says trying to lighten the situation.

John replies in a faint and strangled voice, 'Sorry about this, I must have done something to my back playing Badminton,' he replies.

'Well just lie there, and don't move, in case you make things worse ok.' 'Will you be alright to land this thing on your own,' John remarks. 'Of course I will, no problems,' Martin replies, and at the same time the thought of landing hadn't crossed his mind until then.

Lisbon Air Traffic Controller calls hawk two seven five. Oh my God, Stuart thinks, Lisbon is calling, I had better tell Martin. He gets out of his seat and opens the cabin door, and sees Martin in the galley.

'Lisbon is calling,' he says. 'Right, I'll be right with you,' Martin says, as Stuart hears Lisbon calling again. Should I answer it, they like to be answered straight away, he thinks to himself. No, I had better not, Martin told me not to touch anything, but just let him know when they called.

Martin enters the cabin as Lisbon calls again, only more anxious this time for a reply.

'Hawk to seven five go ahead,' Martin says, as he reaches down and switches the radio transmitter switch on, on his control column.

'Hawk two seven five, message passed to Faro, they will have medics available when you land.' 'Yes, thank you for that, I'll keep you posted should the situation change,' Martin informs Lisbon Air Traffic Controller.

Chapter 23

Tricia looks down the isle and sees all the confusion going on up front. 'I wonder what on earth's going on up there?' she says to Claire. 'I don't know, but it sounded like someone was in a great deal of pain,' she remarks.

'Your Dad is still on the Flight Deck as well. I wish he would hurry up and come and tell us what's going on.'

'Thanks for that,' Martin says to Stuart. 'Oh that's ok, it was the least I could do under the circumstances.' 'There's not a lot you can do for a slipped disc is there?'
'No, I suppose not. I think I should be getting back to my seat. I have delayed you long enough,' Stuart says.

'You needn't, you can stay here if you like, and your wife knows where you are doesn't she?' 'Oh yes.'

'Has anything like this ever happened before?' Stuart asks.

'No, not to my knowledge, but you do get allsorts of different medical emergencies from time to time,' Martin adds, as the cabin door opens and Zoe enters the flighdeck.

'Oh how's the patient?' Martin asks. 'He's been as good as gold. I have just given him some painkillers, and wrapped him in a blanket to keep him warm,' Zoe says, 'Do you want some coffee while things are quiet?' 'Yes please. Do you want some?' Martin asks Stuart. 'Yes please. Could you also tell my wife Tricia I will be staying in here for a little while longer, she's in row twenty?' 'Yes of course.' Zoe leaves the cabin and makes her way down the plane to row twenty to tell Tricia what's happened.

Zoe reaches Tricia, who looks up at her wondering what she was about to say, as Zoe squats down and speaks to her in a quiet voice so as not to be overheard.

'Tricia?' Zoe says. 'Yes,' she replied.

'We have had a medical emergency; the Co Pilot John has slipped a disc in his back, and is unable to move. Stuart has asked me to tell you he will be staying a short while in the cabin before he returns to his seat, so you are not to worry about him, Ok.'

'Yes that's fine, but what about John?' she asks. 'Well I have given him some painkillers, and he is comfortable.' 'Oh good,' Tricia replies as Zoe gets up, and smiles as she makes her way back to the galley to get the coffees for Martin and Stuart.

'Where are we?' Stuart asks Martin. Martin looks at the flight plan display screen and sees they are approaching Mirandela North East of Porto.

'We are approaching a place called Mirandela just North East of Porto.' 'Oh I see,' Stuart replies.

'Have you ever been to Porto?' Martin asks. 'No, have you?' 'No, but I have been to Lisbon. Now that's a nice place for a Holiday. Full of history and culture. The Greeks set up a port there around one thousand two hundred BC. Julius Caesar lived there for a while. Vasco de Gama sailed from there. They had a bad earthquake in the seventeen hundreds, and it was virtually rebuilt after that. It's got some fantastic Palaces and a bridge, one of which is two kilometres long, and was inspired by the Golden Gate Bridge in San Francisco. There's a statue of Christ called the Cristo Rei monument, overlooking the River Tagus and stands some eighty-two meters high. There are plenty of good places to eat, and stay, and I would fully recommend you visit it sometime,' Martin says. 'Yes, I think we should, it sounds an interesting place,' Stuart adds.

Zoe enters the cabin with two coffees for them. 'Thanks,' Martin says, as she hands them a cup each.

'I've told your Wife where you are.' 'Oh thanks,' Stuart replies. They both take a sip of their coffees.

Martin watches the flight display screen, and sees they are about five minutes away from the next reporting point at Viseu.

'Is it me, or is it warm in here?' Martin asks Stuart.

'It seems ok to me,' Stuart replies. 'Well I feel warm.'

'It could be the coffee.' 'Yes, I suppose it could.'

'Undo another button on your shirt,' said Stuart, as Martin reaches to undo another button.

'I really don't feel very well at all,' he says. Martin gets his handkerchief out and wipes his brow, which has started to perspire and run down his face.

Suddenly Martin slams his fist to his chest, as he feels strong pains and pressure. The pain gets worse. Stuart sees he seems to be in a great deal of distress.

'Are you alright?' he asks.

Martin is doubled up now with the pain, which is crushing him inside his chest. He lurches backwards in his seat, but the pain is excruciating, and he slumps forward unconscious over the flight column.

Oh my God, Stuart thinks to himself, as he struggles out of his seat, and reaches for the cabin door, and opens it. He sees Zoe in the galley. 'It's Martin,' he whispers not wishing to attract too much attention to Martin's dilemma.

'He's collapsed.' Stuart looks at a young man sitting on the first seat on the port side. He looks very athletic, and is very tall and slim.

'Quick, give us a hand will you,' Stuart says, as he goes back into the cockpit and bangs the cabin door.

He reaches over to Martin, grabs him under his armpits, and starts to heave him out of his seat. He is very heavy, and the lift angle is not quite right to get the best grip, he struggles, and heaves him up as the young man enters the cabin.

'Quick, grab an arm,' Stuart says as the young man reaches Martin, and they pull together, but Martins foot gets stuck under the flight column.

'Hold him, his foot's stuck.'

Stuart reaches over and pulls his leg clear, and the young man hauls Martin out of his seat. They start to drag him out of the cockpit. They clear the doorway, just as Hawk two seven five reaches Viseu, and makes its computerised left turn, and banks to the left onto the track for Faro. Stuart loses his balance, and with the fact he his still hanging on to Martin, he falls against the toilet door with some force. He bangs his head hard against the doorframe and blacks out, dropping Martin to the floor, as he falls on top of him, causing the young man to fall as well.

Everyone on board witnesses the pile of bodies and the confusion. Screams of panic are heard coming from the rear of the plane.

The young man manages to pull himself up, and drags Martin clear of the doorway into the central isle, well out of sight of the galley. Zoe realises she has a major situation on her hands, and grabs the tannoy microphone, and asks if there is a doctor on board.

The young lady who was sitting infront of Stuart with the two young girls gets up from her seat, and calmly makes her way to the front of the plane.

'Can I help, I am a Doctor?' the lady says, as she reaches Martin.

'Yes if you would,' Zoe says.

The doctor kneels down by Martins head and says, 'What's his name?'
'Martin,' Zoe replies.

'Martin, can you hear me?' There is no reply.

She pinches the skin on his face, but there is still no response. The doctor looks
at his chest, and sees it is rising and falling at a steady rate. She places two
fingers on the right side of his neck on his carotid artery, and feels there is a
pulse, not very strong, but never the less a pulse.

'He's unconscious, can we move him to the back of the plane where there is
more space, and we can place him in the recovery position. I think he may well
have had an Angina attack.'

She gets up from the floor, and Zoe asks four male passengers if they could carry
Martin. Two volunteers take an arm each and a leg each, and they carry him to
the back of the plane.

The doctor returns to her seat, and opens her handbag, and takes out two items.
Then she makes her way to the front of the plane to where Stuart was lying.

She opens a small bottle, and passes it across Stuart's nose, and suddenly he
wakes up with the aid of the smelling salts she had.

'How are you feeling?' she asks, as Stuart gets his bearings. 'Oh, I am fine.
What happened?' 'You banged your head against the door. I have just brought
you round with some smelling salts; feel free to get up when you are feeling ok. I
am just going to the back of the plane if you need anything.' 'Yes thanks,'
Stuart replies, as the doctor makes her way calmly to the rear of the plane.

Tricia, having seen the commotion, leaves her seat and dashes forward to Stuart.
'Are you alright?' she asks, kneeling down to him. 'Yes I am fine, I've just
banged my head, I'll be alright in a minute, don't fuss.'

Martin has been placed in the recovery position, and is lying on his right side.
The doctor kneels down and opens Martins mouth, and lifts up his tongue, and
sprays some liquid into his mouth under his tongue.

'That should work in a few seconds. I have given him Glyceryl Trinitrate. It
will dilate the heart arteries and relieve the attack,' she says.

'Your lucky, I had some in my handbag, only it's an aerosol can, and I thought
about it at the last minute when I was packing, I thought I had better have that
on me, and not in the hold,' she added to Zoe. 'I am glad you did.'

'He may experience a bit of a headache, and dizziness, and possibly an increase in heart rate, but he seems a strong young man, and he should be alright, but no more flying for him today I am afraid. We must get him to Hospital as soon as we can.'

'Oh my God, who's flying the plane?' Zoe says in a state of panic.

'Well the Captain is isn't he?' The doctor says. 'No,' Zoe replies.

'He's the Captain,' as she points down to Martin.

'Well you have two Pilots don't you?' 'Yes, but the other one has slipped the disc in his back, and is recovering on the galley floor.'

'Oh we are in trouble then,' the doctor says in a calm authoritative manner as she looks up at Zoe.

The doctor sees Martin has now opened his eyes. 'I am Doctor Sandra Love. You have had an Angina attack. I have given you something to relieve it. You will be alright, but I want you to rest, so just lie there for a while, and then we will slowly sit you up.' Martin does as he is told for a few seconds, and suddenly he asks.

'Who's flying the plane?' But before the doctor could interject with any comment Zoe snaps back. 'John is. He has recovered, and has taken over control, everything is ok, there is nothing to worry about.' 'Emma stay with Martin will you, I am just going to check on something.'

Zoe leaves the rear of the plane, and makes her way forward towards the galley, and sees Stuart has now got to his feet. He sees John lying on the floor, and he still seems to be in some pain. He goes to speak to John, and to tell him about the incident with Martin, but he can't see Martin anywhere.

Tricia sees that Stuart has now recovered from his fall, and returns to her seat, and as she leaves him she says 'Now don't be long will you?' 'No, I just want to check on John,' he says.

Zoe reaches the galley, and just as Stuart was about to speak to John, she interrupts him. 'Is everything alright here?' 'Yes,' John replies.

'Where's Martin?' he asks. 'Oh he's flying the plane as normal. I was wondering if you would mind if Stuart took him a cup of coffee?'

Stuart looks at Zoe in a bewildered state, as Zoe reaches over to the coffee jug and pours some into a cup.

'Take that through to him will you?' She hands the coffee to Stuart. 'I'll open the door for you.'

They both make their way to the cabin door, and Zoe opens it for Stuart to enter. He steps inside and looks round, and expects to see Martin there, but the flight deck is like the Mary Celeste.

'There's no one here,' he says, as Zoe closes the door behind him.

'Keep your voice down; I don't want every body to know. I know Martin isn't here, he's at the back of the plane, and he has had an Angina attack, and is out of commission. So it's all yours now baby.'

'What do you mean?' 'I mean you are now the Captain.'

'I can't fly the plane. I have never flown a plane in my life.'

'Well NOW's the time to learn. You've flown a Flight Simulator haven't you?'

'Yes, but it's not like this.'

'Well I don't want to make a too finer point about this, but lets put it this way, there are one hundred and fifty people out there who are expecting our spare Pilot to take over in a crisis, got it.'

'No, you can't do this to me.' 'Sorry, but lets put it this way, what have you got to lose.'

Stuart suddenly realises the gravity of the situation. 'I shall want some help from you, so don't think you're getting away with it.'

'No, you are right, I will help, but I must go and let Emma and Chris know what's happening.'

Zoe leaves Stuart in the cabin and enters the passenger area. She sees what appears to be a mutiny amongst the passengers, with several people standing up and talking, and several people around Emma, who has stepped away from Martin, and is about three-quarters of the way down the isle. I had better get this situation under control and quick, she thinks to herself, as she makes her way to the back.

'What's happening?' someone asked, as she makes her way along the isle. She ignores the comment, and continues, until she reaches the group of people milling around Emma.

'Now what's all the excitement,' she says, as she gets closer. One of the group, a big burly man in his early thirties, with tattoos on his arm says, 'What's going on. We want some answers, and quick. We've got women and kids here you know, and babies.'

'Well Sir, we do have a situation, of which you are well aware of, but there is no need to worry at all, our spare Pilot is flying the plane, and everything is under control. So please calm down and return to your seats, we shall be landing shortly.'

The commotion breaks up, and the passengers return to their seats, and begin to pass on the message about the spare Pilot.

Emma is completely confused now. 'What spare Pilot?' she asks Zoe in a very soft voice, as she whispers the remark into her ear.

'Stuart,' Zoe replies.

'Whose Stuart?' 'The chap who has been visiting the Cockpit with John.'

'But he's a passenger.' 'I know.'

'So how's he going to land this damn plane?' 'I don't know, but I don't want this lot knowing about that fact. So keep quiet, and I mean quiet. I don't want John or Martin knowing what's going on, get it?'

'Oh yes.' 'Yes and you and Chris will be in charge out here, and when you hear me say over the intercom Flight Attendants to their seats, start to make sure everyone is fastened in, and in the braced position for crash landing.'

'Oh my God.' 'Let's hope it doesn't come to that, but lets be prepared, and do it discreetly, I don't want a major panic situation arising out of this.' 'And where will you be while all this fun is going on?' 'I shall be assisting Stuart.' 'Right,' Emma says.

Zoe makes her way forward again smiling as she passes everyone giving an air of confidence to the passengers as she passes down the isle.

Chapter 24

'Hawk two seven five,' the Lisbon ATC called. Still there was no response. Stuart hears the radio going again. Oh my God, I had better do something, he thinks to himself, as he realises everything from now on is down to him. 'Hawk two seven five,' Lisbon calls yet again. Stuart struggles into the captains' seat and picks up the headset, and puts it on, and throws the radio switch over to transmission. 'Hawk two seven five,' Stuart says. 'Hawk two seven five, we have been calling you for sometime, is everything all right?' 'I am afraid not,' Stuart says, 'The Captain has had an Angina attack, he collapsed unconscious, and had to be dragged out of the Cockpit. You already know about the Co Pilot.' 'So who's flying the plane?' 'I am,' Stuart replies. 'And who are you?' The ATC controller in Lisbon asks. 'I am a passenger, and my name is Stuart Osborn, and I was sitting in row twenty. The First Officer John Cutler had invited me into the Cockpit, when this lot cracked off,' Stuart replies.

'I see,' the controller said in Lisbon, and at the same time he motioned by hand to his line manager to come over to his desk. 'We have a serious situation with flight MAM two seven five from Birmingham to Faro. Both flight deck crewmembers have been taken seriously ill, and the plane is being flown by a passenger,' the controller says.

'Ok, I'll get onto Faro and warn them of the situation, you keep him talking, and find out as much as you can about his flying abilities,' the line manager said. 'Someone is going to need all the help they can get,' he added, as he went to his office to make the call to Faro.

'Hawk two seven five,' the controller called. 'Hawk two seven five,' Stuart replied. 'So Stuart,' the controller said, 'how much flying experience have you?' he asked. 'None, well I have flown a Cessna one five two for a couple of minutes, and I have a Flight Simulator with this type of aircraft on, but I have never actually flown a plane properly,' he said.

'Don't worry everything will be ok, these planes will almost fly themselves. Anyway I shall be handing you over to Faro soon, and they will talk you down.'

'Yes thanks for that,' Stuart replied, 'I know I should feel very worried, but at this moment in time I feel quite happy about things,' he added.

'Good, you sound calm, and you will need all that calmness later, but we will be with you. How many are on board?' The controller asked.
'I think there are about one hundred and fifty passengers and five crewmembers,' Stuart replied. 'Ok. I will advise you in a minute the radio frequency to change to, to contact Faro.' 'Ok,' Stuart replies.

A young businessman in his mid thirties, with dark hair, and wearing a white shirt and grey trousers, and of a smart appearance, seemed to have noticed far more of the events which had taken place, than many of the other passengers had. He was sitting behind Stuart in row twenty-one, and despite the fact mobile phones were banned from use on a plane, he was determined to inform his wife, who was due to meet him at Faro Airport, of the situation he believed was taking place.

He opened his phone and sent a Text message to her. TROUBLE ON PLANE MAY BE LATE. I THINK A PASSENGER IS FLYING THE PLANE. He pressed the send key, and sent the message. He then switched off the phone, and put it in his shirt pocket.

Faro airport is a relatively quiet airport, compared to many others, and is mainly busy with holiday traffic in the summer season.

The businessman's wife, who was also in her mid thirties, and wearing a pale yellow tee shirt, and beige skirt, was standing by the arrival entrance at the airport. She was keeping out of the sun and the heat of the day, waiting for the arrival of flight MAM two seven five from Birmingham, when her mobile phone bleeped.

She opened the phone and saw it was a text message from her husband, and she read it. 'Oh my God,' she said out loud, and gasped at the same time, and put her hand to her mouth in order to suppress the words she had said. Oh my God, what shall I do now, she thought to herself, and looked around the arrivals hall, but still not sure of what she should do, and whether anyone else knew anything about flight MAM two seven five from Birmingham.

Her pulse raced, and she felt quite sick inside. Now come on gal, she thought to herself, think, go on ask at the information desk, and she started to make her way across the hall. Walking normally at first, then she started to trot, and finally she found herself running very fast as she hit the desk with some force. 'What's happening to flight MAM two seven five?' she blurted out in a loud voice, interrupting the conversation with the clerk, and another passenger.

The clerk stopped her conversation with the passenger, and looked dumfounded at the lady, as she didn't have a clue what she was talking about. 'Flight MAM two seven five from Birmingham is in trouble. I have just had a message from my Husband who is on that plane. So what's going on?' 'Excuse me,' the clerk said to the passenger. 'I am sorry madam, but I don't know what you are talking about, but I will try and find out for you.'

She picked up the telephone under the counter and rang the control tower. The telephone is answered. 'Tower,' a male voice said. 'This is the information desk down stairs. Someone has just asked me if there is any trouble with flight MAM two seven five from Birmingham?' 'We are just getting reports the planes flight crew have been taken seriously ill, and the plane is being flown by a passenger. That's as much as we know at the moment. We are about to be handed over to the plane in a few minutes. How does your customer know more than we do at this stage?' the controller asked. 'She has had a message from her Husband who is on the plane,' the clerk replied. 'Well you had better be careful what you say in response, we don't want to cause a panic situation.' 'Yes ok,' the clerk replied, as she put down the phone.

'Well, what did they say?' the lady asked. 'They have told me the situation is well under control, and the plane will be landing on time, and there is nothing to worry about.'

'Nothing to worry about. My Husband said a passenger is flying the plane. You say there is nothing to worry about. Well I disagree lady.'

By now, other people who had been standing near the information desk had overheard the conversation, and they all started to ask the clerk what was going on. 'I've got my Wife and two Kids on that plane so what's going on,' a man at the back of the crowd shouted, desperately trying to make himself heard over the noise and questions, as the situation was now well out of hand.

One of the people in the crowd was a reporter for a local paper. He had overheard the conversation and realised there was a story breaking. He opened his mobile phone and rang his office. 'Put me through to the News Desk,' he said as the switchboard answered his call. 'It's Juan. I am at the Airport, you had better tune into the Air Band Radio, the flight from Birmingham MAM two seven five is in trouble. It appears a passenger is flying it. You had also better hold the front page, and send a photographer down here quick, and contact the TV companies, they might want to send a film crew down here as well. I'll ring you back in a few minutes with some more info.' He switched off his mobile phone, and walked towards the crowd of people now gathered round the information desk. He could see a supervisor had now joined the clerk, and they were both trying to reassure people everything was ok.

'Hey Lady,' one of the passengers in row thirteen on the plane called out to Zoe. 'What's going on?' he asked loudly, standing up in his seat to make his point. Zoe turned round to speak to the passenger, and stepped towards him. Other passengers were now chanting the same question, and she realised the situation was getting out of hand, and something needed to be done to calm things down. 'Quiet John,' the man's wife said, pulling him back down in his seat.

Zoe decided it was time to speak to the passengers, and went to the front of the plane, and picked up the tannoy microphone. The commotion with the passengers shouting at one another was deafening as she shouted down the microphone. 'Quiet.' She waited a short while for the noise to die down. 'Thank you. This is the senior Stewardess speaking. Some of you seem to be concerned about events taking place on the aircraft. I cannot deny we do have a situation, but I can reassure you all, everything is under control. There really is no need to worry. We shall be landing shortly. So please stay calm and enjoy the film, I will find out our time of arrival at Faro. Thank you.' She switched the microphone off, and thought to herself, God, I do hope my nose isn't growing for telling that white lie.

She opened the cockpit door, and stepped inside, and closed the door behind her. She saw Stuart was in the captains' seat with his headphones on. He turned round to her and smiled, 'How are things out there?' he asked. 'How are things in here more to the point. I hope you know what you're doing, because I have just told the biggest white lie in my life out there in order to save a riot with the passengers.'
'It's as bad as that is it,' Stuart said. 'Yes, and if I don't keep them sweet, we shall all be in it big time,' Zoe replied. 'Well, I can't deny I am not too chuffed about things either, but what else can we do. Someone has got to get this thing down without breaking it,' Stuart remarked.

'Have you any idea on our ETA yet,' Zoe asked. 'I think, give or take a few minutes, it should be about half an hour, and that will be more or less on time,' Stuart replied. 'Hawk two seven five,' Lisbon controller called out. 'Lisbon's calling,' Stuart said. 'Ok I will leave you to it, and pray you don't break it,' Zoe said, as she left the cockpit.

She returns to the tannoy microphone and picks it up. 'Sorry to interrupt your film, but I have just spoken with the Pilot, and we should be landing on time in about half an hour. Thank you.' She switches the microphone off, and starts to make her way to the back of the plane to see how Martin is doing.

As she passes Tricia, Tricia reaches out, and grabs Zoë's hand, and pulls her down to speak to her quietly. 'Now what's going on, and no lies this time?' she says to Zoe. 'Stuart and I will be flying the plane.' 'You and Stuart, but he doesn't know a thing about flying,' she says. 'I have every confidence in him, and we will be ok, so don't worry.' 'Don't worry, that's my Husband out there, and you say don't worry. Well I am scared to death.' 'Shush, not so loud. I am trying to avoid a serious panic situation, so please help me, and stay calm for everyone's sake.'

Zoe gets up, and continues to the back of the plane, and has a word with Emma and Chris, and updates them on the situation in the cockpit.

'What did she say Mom?' Claire asks in a quiet whispered voice. 'She says your Dad is flying the plane.' 'Oh my God,' Claire says, gasping, and flopping back in her seat in a state of shock.

Craig looks at his sister and his mom wondering what they were whispering about, but looks out of the window without enquiring on their conversation. Tricia sees him look and she whispers to Claire, 'Don't mention it to Craig will you?' 'No,' Claire replies.

My God, I hope you know what you are doing, Tricia thinks to herself, and praying Stuart doesn't cock things up, or they will all be killed.

'Hawk two seven five,' the Lisbon controller called out. Stuart answered. 'Hawk two seven five.' 'Would you now change to the Faro approach frequency on one one nine point four, they are expecting your call, and they are aware of your situation.' ' One one nine point four will do, but how do I do that?' Stuart asks. 'Can you see the Radio stack in the centre Console area?' 'Yes.' 'Well the top windows are for the Radio Transmitter. If you turn the dial until the reading changes to one one nine point four you will be able to speak to Faro, Ok.' 'Yes and thanks for your help,' Stuart replied. 'Good luck,' the controller added. Having set the frequency he called out to Faro.

'Faro this is Hawk two seven five.' 'Hawk two seven five, this is Faro approach.' The female voice replied in a calm tone, 'We have you on Radar, but would you please set the squawk frequency on your Transponder to two three six five.' 'Yes I can, but where is the Transponder frequency?' Stuart asked. 'It's at the bottom of the radio panel. If you dial in the numbers I have given you, and then press the Ident button, we will pick up the signal.'

Stuart identifies the transponder panel, and selects the frequency of two three six five, and presses the Ident button. 'I have done that,' Stuart says to the controller. 'Yes we are getting you,' the controller added. 'Good,' Stuart replied. 'Now in a few minutes you will see two Fighter planes come and join you. Don't worry, they won't be coming to shoot you down, they will be there to assist you, and reassure you. We will begin to prepare you to descend. We shall also require you to change heading onto a one six zero heading, but I shall talk you through each bit slowly, and we shall do one thing at a time.' 'Yes ok,' Stuart replied.

'I shall be handing you over to a qualified seven three seven Pilot who will converse with you, and talk you down, she is English, and her name is Kate.' 'Yes, thanks for that, it should make life easy for me,' Stuart replied.

Ring, Ring, Ring the phone rang in the airport managers office, a hand reaches down and picks up the phone. 'Hello,' 'This is security,' the voice said in the earpiece. 'We have a serious situation down here, I think you should come down.' 'Why, what's the matter?' 'A crowd has built up, and the press, and film crews have arrived. It seems we have a plane coming in, which is being flown by a passenger, and they have come to film it.' 'Right, I will be down in a minute.' The manager puts the phone down, and makes his way downstairs. As he arrives at the main foyer he sees the melee of people, and the information desk seemed to be besieged. He sees the head of security is standing watching what was going on. The manager walks towards him when one of the people in the crowd, a reporter for the local paper, recognises the manager and rushes across to him. 'What's going on?' the reporter asked as he reached him. By now, several other people came over to him as well. 'I have spoken to the Air Traffic Controllers, and the situation is well under control, so why don't you all give the staff a break, and let them get on with their jobs.' He puts his arms out in an attempt to usher the people back, and away from the information desk.

'Hey we are not being palmed off with any fob story from you, we want to know what's going on. I've got my Wife and Kids on that plane,' a voice in the crowd shouted out. 'Yes come on, give us a break, and fill us in,' a reporter shouted.

'It seems we have a situation where the flight crew have been taken ill, and one of the passengers is flying the plane, but all help is being given to him by our Air Traffic Controllers, and I am afraid that's as much as we can say at the moment.' 'Is it going to crash?' one of the reporters asked. 'We hope not, but of course we can't rule it out. As I said, we do have a situation, which we hope will have good results in the end. Now please, I must attend to other matters, but feel free to go to the viewing lounge if you wish.' With that, the crowd rushed to the viewing lounge to get the best possible viewing position. One of the film crews and their reporter leave the building, and make for a better viewing position outside closer to the runway.

The manager walks across to the head of security 'Can you get as many of your people in here, and get some security barriers across to stop this happening again, and try and keep them in some sort of order?' 'Yes ok.'

136

Chapter 25

'Hawk two seven five, this is Kate talking to you now.' 'Hi, pleased to meet you,' Stuart replied. 'What's your current flight level and heading?' she asked. 'Hawk two seven five, flight level three two zero heading one eight six,' Stuart called back. 'Yes thank you for that. I will be requiring you to make a left turn onto heading one six zero in about three minute's time, can you do that?' Kate asked. 'Yes heading one six zero,' Stuart replied. 'After that I want you to slow the speed of the plane down, and then I shall ask you to start to reduce height. Do you think you will be able to do that?' She said. 'Yes,' Stuart replied.

'You will find you have company in a few minutes in the form of two F 16 Military Planes who are there to reassure you of the situation you are in, Ok.' 'Yes,' Stuart replied. 'Now, on the panel infront of you, on the top edge, you should see four window display panels. One is marked Course, the other is marked Nav, and there are some buttons underneath, and one should have HDG above it.' 'Yes, do you want me to press the button, and readjust the heading to one six zero from one eight six.' 'Yes, but first of all I want you to set the heading bug to one eight six, your current heading before you commence the change. Because the plane is flying on its computerised flight route, we will need to get you out of this onto a more manual control.' 'Will do,' Stuart replies, and commences to alter the setting. 'Done that.' 'Right, now infront of you on that upper edge, you should see a switch marked Nav/Course. Switch it to Nav.' Stuart flicks the switch to Nav. 'Done that,' he says to Kate.

'Right, you can now make that left turn onto heading one six zero, so press the Heading Bug Button.' Stuart reaches up to the panel and presses the button, and turns the panel numbers round to one six zero, and presses the button again, and the plane immediately turns to the left, onto the heading of one six zero, and levels off on that heading. 'Heading one six zero,' Stuart says. ' Yes great, now reduce speed to two fifty knots. If you look to the top left of the panels infront of you, you can see the Airspeed Indicator dial and at the bottom left corner is a small knob, turn it one way or the other slowly, and reduce the speed of the aircraft to two fifty knots.' Stuart again reaches up to the panel infront of him, and turns the knob reducing the speed on the IAS panel (Indicated Air Speed) and reduces the speed to two fifty knots. As the plane is flying on the autopilot, the auto throttles automatically move the throttle levers back, and the engines are heard to reduce their revolutions, as the speed on the Airspeed Indicator dial starts to come down to the set red line marker at two fifty knots.

Stuart is suddenly aware of the two F16 fighter aircraft of the Portuguese Air force are now alongside him. 'The Fighters are with me now,' Stuart says. 'Yes, we have you all together on our screens,' Kate replies.

Craig sees the fighter planes from his window seat. 'Mom look,' he says in an excited manner, as he attracts his mother and sisters attention to the window, and they both look out, and see one of the fighter aircraft flying alongside them, and level with the front of the aeroplane. 'Oh my God,' Tricia gasps, and Claire grabs her hand, and squeezes it tight. 'Oh yes, that's nice,' Tricia says to Craig fearing the worst at the same time.

'I can see the man's face, he is waving to us.' 'How nice,' Tricia says, shaking like a leaf, and trying to keep calm, and yet holding back her tears.

Everyone on the plane has now seen the two fighter planes alongside them, and voices are now being raised as the conversation between the passengers gets louder, as they wonder why the planes are so close.

'Are you ready now to commence your descent?' Kate asks Stuart. 'Yes I am ready when you are,' he replies. 'Ok, go to the panel infront of you again, and on the right hand side you should see the Altitude setting reading thirty two thousand feet.' 'Yes I see it.' 'Release the button underneath it.' 'Yes done that.' 'You can now reduce the numbers to twenty five thousand feet.' 'Yes,' Stuart replies, and at the same time redials twenty five thousand feet. He presses the altitude button again, and the plane starts to dip the nose down, and the altimeter starts to go round anti clockwise, and the numbers in the middle of the dial start to reduce as the plane commences its descent. The two fighter planes follow the aircraft down.

'We're going down,' Craig says to his mother. Tricia and Claire squeeze each other's hand tight as Tricia's stress levels start to rise as she begins to fear the worst.

Stuart monitors the altimeter as the cabin door opens, and Zoe enters the cabin. 'I see we have company,' she says to Stuart. 'Yes, they have been there a couple of minutes now. Are you coming to help me?' 'Yes if you like. Emma and Chris are aware of what's going on, and I have left Emma in charge for a while. What do you want me to do?' 'Sit in the Co Pilots seat, and put the Headphones on, and listen to the Radio with me, so I don't make a mistake on the instructions when they come, Ok.' 'Yes,' Zoe replies, and she climbs into the co pilot's seat, and puts the headphones on.

Stuart sees the altimeter pass twenty seven thousand feet. 'The descent will stop in a few seconds,' he says to Zoe. It passes twenty six thousand feet, and Stuart watches the dial intently, and starts to count the feet in the hundreds. 'Eight, seven, six, five, four, three, two, one, zero.' The indicator passes the twenty five thousand feet mark, but the planes nose stops descending, and rises to the level position, and the indicator goes back and settles at twenty five thousand feet. 'We made it,' Stuart says, and sighs with relief as the auto throttles move automatically forward, and the engines revs rise slightly and level off.

'We are now at flight level two five zero,' Stuart says to Kate. 'Good remain there, and I will get you to descend to fifteen thousand feet, or as you seem to like flight level one five zero in a couple of minutes.'

Suddenly the plane starts to shake, and bounce around. The passengers start to scream. The sudden, and unexpected movement of the aircraft startles Tricia, but it only lasts for a few seconds. 'That was a bit of turbulence; I was wondering when we might get some. It's nothing to worry about; I'll just put the seat belt sign on. Can you tell the passengers its only turbulence, and there is nothing to worry about, and to put their seat belts on for safety,' Stuart says to Zoe.

'How do I do that?' Zoe asks. 'Can you see that switch on the Flight Column, it's got Rad and PA?' 'Yes.' 'Well flick to PA and speak like you do on the Tannoy.' 'Oh Yes Ok,' Zoe flicks the switch. 'This is Senior Flight Attendant, we are experiencing some turbulence, it's nothing to worry about, but for safety reasons, and your comfort, would you please put your Seat Belts on, thank you.' She switches the switch back, and ends the transmission. 'That should keep them quiet for a bit,' Stuart says.

He then looks out of the window to his left, and sees the fighter pilot put his thumb up to him, approving of the descent he had just made. Stuart puts his thumb back up to him and smiles, and then puts his fingers in his mouth and bites them in a nervous gesture. The fighter pilot wipes his forehead, and flicks his hand in a light-hearted response, and they both smile at each other.

'Hawk two seven five, descend to flight level one five zero.' 'Descending to flight level one five zero,' Stuart replies, as he repeats the procedure he did when he descended to flight level two five zero. The plane starts to descend again.

'Hawk two seven five, while you are descending I want you to do some changes on your Radio Panel, and to set the ADF (Automatic Direction Finder) and Navigation frequency settings, Ok.' 'Yes,' Stuart replies. 'Right, lets first set the ADF frequency. Go to the Radio Panel and the fourth panel down, and you will see three knobs, turn them one way or the other, and enter three three two. You should see a blue arrow on the VOR (VHF Omni Directional Range) ADF display come on infront of you. Make sure the little switch at the bottom is pointing towards the ADF sign before you start to make the changes. Let me know when you have done this.' 'Yes ok.'

Stuart begins to make the changes, having made sure the switch was pointing to the ADF setting, and as he completes the changes, the blue arrow appears, and points to his right. 'Done it,' he replies. 'As you can see it is pointing to the right, it is pointing towards the Airfield, so you should always be aware where it is.' 'Yes Ok.' 'This is the Non Directional Beacon, and it is situated one nautical mile from the runway threshold, and you will pass over it when you come in to land, but don't worry about that now. I have just told you this for your information, Ok.' 'Yes, I am with you.'

'Right, I now want you to set the Navigation frequency. You can see on the Radio Panel again Nav one and Nav two. Again they have knobs to change the settings, so I want you to set Nav one to frequency one one two point eight, Ok.' 'Yes doing it now, done it,' he replied. 'Now we have to set the Course setting. Can you see the first window on the upper Dashboard infront of you?' 'Yes.' 'Well that is the course setting I want you to change. Will you now change the reading to two eight three, and tell me when you have done this?' 'Doing it now,' Stuart replies as he starts to change the number. At the same time the compass dial on the H S I (Horizontal Situation Indicator) display screen infront of him starts to turn to the right, and stops as he reaches the setting of two eight three. 'Done that,' Stuart says over the radio to Faro. 'Right, now that is set three degrees to the left of the Runway, and when you are one point six miles from the threshold, you will turn right three degrees, onto a heading of two eight six to line up with the Runway. You should also now have an off set bar being shown in the middle of the H S I display screen infront of you. Can you see it?' 'Yes.' 'Well, that bar will move towards the middle the nearer you get to the Airfield. How are you doing for height?' 'I am just about to level off at flight level one five zero.' 'Right, remain on the heading, and descend to flight level one one zero, and reduce speed to two forty knots, and let me know when you have done them.' 'Yes descending to flight level one one zero and reducing speed to two forty knots.'

The plane starts its descent. 'Hey, we're not doing too bad so far are we,' Stuart says to Zoe. 'I think you are brilliant.' 'I wouldn't go so far as to say that. Wait until we get nearer the Airfield. That's what I am not looking forward to.' 'I couldn't do what you have just done, you make me feel so safe.'

Stuart looks out of the port side window and sees the pilot of the F16 on his left wave his hand, and at the same time points down, and then suddenly he turns left away from the aircraft, and descends very fast away from them.

'The Fighters have left us for a while,' Stuart says to Zoe as she looks out of her window, and sees the fighter plane on her side disappear to her right. 'I don't think we have seen the last of them,' Stuart remarks.

'Gosh Mom, the Fighter Planes gone,' Craig says in an excited manner. 'Why are the Fighter Planes up here Mom?' 'I don't know,' Tricia replies. 'Where's Dad?' 'He is helping the man fly the plane.' 'Why?' 'God you can get on peoples nerves sometimes with all your questions, now give Mom a break, and keep looking to make sure the engine is still there, and stop annoying people,' Claire says.

'Level at flight level one one zero speed two forty knots,' Stuart says to Kate.

'You should see the coast infront of you now. We are going to send you out to sea for a while to give you time to lose height, and prepare for the landing, so don't worry. On the centre Console infront of you, you should see the GPS, Ground Positioning System display screen.' 'Yes I can see it.' 'Well as you will see, it shows you exactly where you are, and where we are, and the outline of the coast infront of you.' 'Yes,' 'Is that of help to you?' 'Yes, no problems, I have been keeping an eye on it for sometime.' 'Good, now I want you to descend to flight level three zero and reduce speed to two ten knots. We reckon you should cross the coast at about flight level four zero. I also want you to change the Radio frequency to one one eight point two, also press the APR button to engage the automatic approach.' 'Yes got all that.'

Chapter 26

'Quiet you lot, I can't hear the Radio.' The chief editor at the local paper says, as he tries to listen to the radio, which is being drowned by the chatter in the office. He hears part of the conversation between Stuart and Faro, and only gets the bit about them heading out to sea. He jumps to the conclusion the plane is going to crash out at sea. He picks up his telephone and phones his reporter at the airport.

'Yes', the Reporter says, as he answers his phone. 'It looks like they are going to crash the plane out at sea. Find out what's going on will you,' the editor says.

'Are you sure you have heard right, they are going to crash the plane at sea?' the reporter asks, but his conversation is overheard by people standing nearby. 'They are going to crash into the sea,' someone in the crowd shouts, as the panic starts to spread rapidly amongst the anxious crowd waiting the fate of their loved ones.

In desperation to warn her husband of the fate of the plane, she texts him of the news, just as he opens his mobile phone to text her, they will be landing shortly.

He can't believe what he has just read on the text message, and he shouts out, 'We're going to crash in the sea.'

People scream, and start to cry, as the news spreads through the plane. Emma rushes forward to the cockpit to speak with Zoe. She bursts into the cockpit, which frightens the life out of Stuart and Zoe. 'Is it true, are we going to crash into the Sea?' Emma says, in a fleet of panic.

At the same time the plane banks to its right, as the autopilot turns the plane towards the airfield at Faro. More screams are heard from within the plane as Stuart replies 'No, we are about to land. Now get back there, and reassure everybody everything is ok.' Emma leaves the cockpit, and closes the door behind her.

'Hawk two seven five,' Kate calls. 'Hawk two seven five,' Stuart replies.

'Reduce speed to one eight zero knots, and lower the undercarriage.'
'Reducing speed to one eight zero knots and lowering the undercarriage.'

He reduces the speed, and reaches across to the right hand side of the console, and pulls the undercarriage lever down. He waits a few seconds, and watches for the three green lights to show, indicating the undercarriage is down, but only two lights come on, the nose wheel light fails to illuminate.

'Hawk two seven five,' Stuart calls Faro.

'Hawk two seven five,' Faro replies. 'The Nose Wheel Light for the Undercarriage hasn't illuminated.'

'Ok, don't worry about it; it's probably an electrical fault. We'll observe you as you approach, to confirm if the wheel is locked down. Now set the Flaps to five degrees.'

'Setting Flaps five degrees.' Stuart reaches across the throttle levers to the flap lever, and pulls it down to the five degrees setting.

Emma speaks to the passengers on the tannoy, in order to reassure them all is well, and they are about to land.

Tricia turns to Claire. 'I hope to God that man is wrong about us crashing into the sea.' Claire looks out of the window and sees land approaching again. 'I don't think we are, I can see land again down there.' 'Thank God for that,' Tricia says.

As the situation seems to be doomed, the businessman feels he should send his last message to his wife Marie at the airport, as he feels sure the plane will crash, and he will never see her again.

He opens his phone and text's, I LOVE YOU SO MUCH REMEMBER ME ALWAYS. He presses the send button, and closes the phone, and replaces it in his shirt pocket. He puts his head back on the headrest and closes his eyes, and thinks of the day in late summer when they met on the beach in their late teens. How they lay there on the sand, and how he looked into her face, as she lay asleep in the sun, with a radiant smile. Having been in the sea, her wet dark hair was shining in the sunlight. How much in love with her he was then, and still is. The words from the song 'Every time I look at you' come to his mind, as he sings them to himself, and the emotion of the words in the song rise in his thoughts, and a tear rolls down his left cheek.

'This is Dan Casper reporting to you live from Faro International Airport for INN.
News is coming in of flight MAM two seven five from Birmingham England, which is in serious trouble. There are one hundred and fifty passengers on board, and five-Flight Crew. Reports are indicating two of the Flight Crew on board, have been taken seriously ill, and the plane is being flown by a passenger. It is possible the plane may be heading out to sea, and the destiny of the passengers and crew looks unsure at this stage. We have spoken to the airport management,

who have reassured us all is well, and the plane will be landing shortly, but messages from passengers on the plane indicate otherwise.'

With that, sirens are heard to be coming from the far side of the airport, and the television camera sees crash tenders and ambulances, as they race from their buildings towards the main runway.

The camera then swings further to the left, and the cameraman zooms out towards the far end of the runway, and three planes can be seen heading towards the airport, and still several miles away.

'Hawk two seven five. I have spoken to the F16 Pilots and they reassure me that the Nose Wheel is locked down.'

'That's nice to know,' Stuart replies.

'Now set the speed to one sixty knots, and lower Flaps to ten degrees,' Kate tells Stuart.

'Setting speed to one sixty knots, and lowering Flaps to ten degrees.'

'Flight Attendants to landing seats,' Stuart calls over the PA to the flight crew. Emma and Chris make their way to their seats at the front of the plane, and at the same time check on every passenger, as they walk down the isle that they have their seat belts fastened.

As they reach the front, Chris takes her seat as Emma picks up the tannoy, and informs the passengers to brace themselves for a bumpy landing, and to assume the crash position.

Anxious fears come to the thoughts of the passengers, as they brace themselves for what might be their last moments on earth. There is a deathly hush inside the plane, as they feel it slow down, and they listen intently to every noise the plane makes, as it approaches the airport.

'Descend now to one thousand feet,' Kate informs Stuart. Stuart reaches across, and reduces the height to one thousand feet, and informs Faro that task has been done.

'Are you strapped in?' Stuart asks Zoe. 'Yes,' she replies, as she notices the F16 planes move further away from them.

'You are now on final approach. How far are you away?' Kate asks.

'Five miles,' Stuart replies.

'In three miles I want you to turn right onto a heading of two eight six.'

'Yes, ok getting ready,' Stuart replies, as he reaches up to the heading bug.

'Now turn onto heading two eight six.' Stuart readjusts the heading setting, and the plane turns right onto the heading.

'Reduce height to five hundred feet.' 'Reducing height to five hundred feet,' Stuart replies.

The plane descends towards the five hundred feet height, and he notices the ADF blue arrow swings to the down position, as he passes over the non-directional beacon. He also looks out of the window, and sees a sewerage farm below him.

'God, I hope we don't land in that stuff,' he says to Zoe.

'Why, what is it?' she says, as she looks out of the window infront.

'It's a Sewerage Farm,' Stuart replies.

'Lets pray we don't,' she says, laughing at the same time.

'Knock off the APR button,' Kate tells Stuart.

'Knocking off the APR button,' Stuart replies.

'Reduce speed to one fifty knots, and set Flaps fifteen degrees, and reduce height to three hundred feet, and do it as quick as you can,' Kate says, in an urgent manner. Stuart commences the task as fast as he can, as the plane is now almost over the threshold of the airfield.

The plane is slow to react. 'Sorry Stuart you are too high, you won't make it. You will have to go round and come in again. So hit the To Go round button on the right of the Throttle Levers, and increase your height back to two thousand feet, but stay on this heading.' 'Will do,' Stuart says as he hits the To Go round button.

'Now decrease Flaps to five degrees, and raise the Undercarriage.' Stuart carries out the task, which is now stressing him out, as he wished the ordeal were over.

'Increase power to two ten knots.' Stuart increases the power, and the nose of the plane starts to rise, and they climb back towards two thousand feet.

On the ground, the television cameraman has been following the plane as it approached the airfield.

'For some reason the Plane has aborted its landing, and is climbing away from the Airport,' Dan Casper says, as the noise of the planes engines are heard to deafen out his commentary, and it is seen to fly away from the airfield.

'One can only imagine what is going through the minds of the passengers on board the plane as it failed to land. We all pray for their souls, as we wait their fate.'

Chapter 27

'Reduce Flaps to zero and maintain climb,' Kate says to Stuart.

'Reducing Flaps to zero, and maintaining,' Stuart replies.

'Well done, we are going to turn you right for another run in. How much fuel have you got left?' 'The Gauges are showing about one ton,' Stuart replies.

'Ok, it should be enough, but we must get you down this time, as there won't be enough fuel left for another run.'

'Levelling off at two thousand feet,' Stuart informs Kate.

'Right, turn right now onto a heading of one six.'

Stuart readjusts the heading to one six degrees, and the plane turns right, and settles onto the heading. The two F16's are still shadowing the plane, and are mirroring his turn, as he heads back in land.

'I have the Airport Manager with me Sam Shutt. Sam can you tell us what's happening?' Dan Casper says, as he points the microphone in his direction.

'It seems the Plane was a little too high as it crossed the threshold of the Airfield, and for safety reasons they aborted the landing,' Sam replied.

'That wouldn't happen if a normal Pilot was flying the Plane, would it?' Dan asked.

'No, but we have someone who has never landed at this Airfield before, and it does happen occasionally,' Sam replies.

'What's going to happen now, baring in mind there are over one hundred and fifty passengers on that Plane?' 'Well, they will be making another approach, and hopefully the Pilot will get the Plane a little lower this time.'

'What do you know about the man who is flying the Plane?' ' Nothing, except I am led to believe he is one of the passengers, and a very brave one at that, and he is getting all the help possible.'

Dan turns to the camera, 'Thank you for that. As you have heard the Pilot is very brave, and we all wait to see if he can save the lives of his fellow passengers.'

'Turn right again onto heading one zero six, and report reaching the Coast,' Kate tells Stuart.

'Right, onto one zero six, and report reaching the Coast,' Stuart replies, as he resets the heading bug.

Emma looks across at Chris and smiles. Chris looks very worried, as she has never experienced anything like this before. All her previous flights and landings have been normal, and she finds the experience very distressing.

'Hawk two seven five.' 'Hawk two seven five,' Stuart replies to Faro.

'We think the problem you had with the landing was the air pressure changed, and we must correct your Altimeter setting to one zero two six millibars, can you do that?' 'Yes, will do,' Stuart replies as he readjusts the altimeter setting, by adjusting the altimeter bug on the bottom left hand corner of the altimeter gauge, directly infront of him. This will correct the height of the aircraft as it approaches the final moments of descent.

Stuart looks down at the PA/ RT button in the lull of radio transmissions, and thinks to himself how he would just love to flick the switch to PA and tell Tricia how much he loves her, and the kids. He fingers the button, as if he was caressing her hand, and running his fingers through her hair. He slides his hand round the flight column as if he was putting them round her waist, but as much as he would love to flick the switch, he can't do it for the sake of all the other passengers onboard. He realises there must be no mistakes this time.

Zoe looks to her right out of the window, and sees the fields and the little villas with their terracotta roofs below, as the plane makes it turn. She thinks how nice it would be to live down there in one of the villas, and to think they haven't a clue of what's going on up here, as they enjoy the peace and sunshine.

Tricia sits with the other passengers' still holding Claire's hand as she thinks to herself; I wish I were in the cockpit with Stuart instead of Zoe. If we were going to die, then it would be nice if we died together. A tear rolled down her face as she closed her eyes and prayed.

'I am approaching the coast,' Stuart says to Kate in Faro. 'Right, now turn right onto heading one nine four and reduce speed to one seventy knots.'

Stuart repeats the instruction back to Kate and commences to readjust the heading to one nine four degrees, as the plane makes its right turn, and the speed is reduced.

Stuart presses the APR button ensuring the plane will fly automatically towards the airfield at the appropriate time.

He is still amazed at the fact how little control the human has over direct flying; the hands on stuff so to speak. As computers and automatic systems carry out so much of the actual flying, he thinks to himself, as the plane completes its turn and settles down.

'Descend to one thousand feet,' Kate says to Stuart. 'Descending to one thousand feet,' Stuart replies as he alters the altimeter setting, and the plane starts to descend. He watches the altimeter dial unwind.

'Lower the Undercarriage,' Kate says, as Stuart repeats the instruction and moves the undercarriage lever down, and hopes the nose wheel light comes on this time. The wheel bay doors open, and the wheels start to extend out of the bays, and he sees the two wing wheel lights come on, and finally the nose wheel light also illuminates, as he feels the bang, as they lock into position.

'Undercarriage lights all on this time,' Stuart informs Kate. 'Well done,' came the reply.

'Set Flaps five degrees.' 'Setting Flaps five degrees,' Stuart replies, as he moves the flap lever to the five-degree position. The motors move the flap slats out to their set position.

Stuart starts to see the bar on the H S I display screen begin to move towards the middle.

'Turn right now onto heading two nine zero.' 'Turning right onto heading two nine zero,' Stuart replies, as he resets the planes heading.

The plane banks over to the right. 'Lets hope it works out ok this time,' Stuart says to Zoe. She looks across at him and smiles, 'I am sure it will.'

Stuart sees the angle of the horizon change, and the view of the sea starts to fill the windows as they make their turn, and eventually the sea view is reduced, as the land and sky become more visible, as the turn is completed.

The perspiration starts to slowly roll down Stuart's face, as the tension of the situation sinks in. His heart rate increases, and he feels his chest pounding, and the adrenaline starts to pump.

They cross the coast, and Stuart can faintly see the airport in the distance.

'Turn left onto heading two eight six, and descend to four hundred feet. Reduce speed to one sixty knots and set Flaps ten degrees.'

Stuart repeats the transmission, and commences to carry out the commands in a prompt fashion, as he's now getting to grips with the flying controls. The plane responds quickly to Stuart's actions, and settles down at the new height and speed.

He watches the DME readings on the GPS screen, and sees he is approaching three miles from the airport. He can clearly make out the runway, and it seems he is in the correct position for landing. He can just make out all the blue flashing lights of the fire engines, and ambulances on the perimeter roadway. I hope to God we don't need their services, he thinks to himself, as they get nearer and nearer to the airport.

'The Planes are now approaching the Airport,' Dan Casper says, as the television camera picks them out in the distance. ' We hope they make it this time, and we pray they do,' he says in a quiet tone, as the camera follows the planes flight towards the airfield.

They are now two point six miles from the airfield. 'Descend to two hundred feet and set the Auto Brakes to the third position,' Kate says to Stuart. 'Descending to two hundred feet setting the Auto Brakes to position three', Stuart replies.

Everyone on board is braced in the crash position, and all is quiet, too quiet in some respects, as they are all hoping the next few minutes pass by without incident.

Please, please God let us get down safely Tricia thinks to herself as she clings onto Claire's hand.

'Set Flaps fifteen degrees and disengage the APR button, and the Altimeter button.' Stuart carries out the instructions quickly. 'Done,' he replies.

'Disengage the I A S button, and move the Throttle levers to idle as you cross the threshold, and let the plane float down, but pull the Flight Column back slightly, to ensure the nose is raised up.' 'Will do,' Stuart replies.

'This is it kid,' Stuart says to Zoe. 'Now brace yourself gal, its shit or bust time,' as Stuart pulls the flight column back slightly as instructed.

Zoe is holding on tight to the side of the co pilots' seat, as she sees the ground coming up faster and faster. Stuart turns the flight column slightly to the right, in order to correct the line up position for the centre of the runway. His heart is now beating like an express train.

'It looks like we have a welcoming Committee,' Stuart says to Zoe, who looks out of the window as they approach the threshold of the runway and she sees the fire engines, and ambulances.

They cross the threshold of the runway, and Stuart moves the throttle levers back to the idle position. The plane floats on down, and he hears the back wheels hit the runway with a thud, and the plane shakes, and rumbles as the wheels settle down after their collision with the tarmac. Curling plumes of blue smoke are seen to rise from the tyres of the plane as the camera follows them along the runway. The plane bumps along the tarmac. The banging is heard, and felt by everyone on board. Stuart then pushes the flight column forward, and the nose of the plane comes down, and he feels the nose wheel hit the ground.

'Yes, we made it,' Zoe shouts. 'Yes, Yes, Yes,' she says, punching the air with her closed fist at the same time. They hear the cheers from the passengers on board.

'Pull the Throttle Levers right back to the reverse thrust position, and steer down the centre of the runway,' Kate says to Stuart.

The throttle levers are pulled right back, and the auto brakes start to bite in, and the plane reduces speed.

The television camera follows the plane, having captured the moment of landing. The noise from the reverse thrusts, and the two F 16 fighters drown any attempt of a commentary from Dan Casper for a few seconds.

'We have just witnessed a perfect landing of flight MAM two seven five despite all the concerns. The man who was flying that Plane must be One Cool Guy. He has my respect for saving the lives of all on board,' Dan says to the viewing public, as the fire engines, and ambulances race along the runway behind the plane, with their sirens whaling, and blue lights flashing.

'Return the Throttles to idle and release the Auto Brakes,' Kate says to Stuart. 'Releasing the brakes, and setting the throttles to idle, and thank you for all your help. I didn't think we were going to make it.'

'Ok you are welcome. I could say anytime, but I hope we don't meet again like this,' Kate replied.

The plane freewheels along the runway towards the far end, and is rolling very slowly as Stuart releases the auto brakes and allows the plane to freewheel to a stop.

'Can you taxi the Plane to the end of the Runway?' 'Yes I think so, I've got it this far, I think I will make the rest,' Stuart replies, as he pushes the throttles forward and slowly increases the speed of the plane. He sets the flaps back to zero, and turns right at the end of the runway, and heads back towards the main terminal along the taxiway.

Zoe releases her seat belt, and climbs out of her seat, and rushes across the cabin, and gives Stuart a kiss on his cheek. 'That's from me, and these are from my kids,' as she commences to kiss him again.

'Ok, I surrender,' Stuart says. 'Right, I shall go and sort this lot out.'

She opens the cabin door, and the noise of cheering passengers was deafening. 'Who loves ya Baby,' she says, as she closes the door.

Having left the runway, Stuart commences his journey along the taxiway towards the main terminal. He sees the 'Follow Me' car with its yellow flashing beacon on, and the driver waving his arm out of the drivers window, signalling Stuart to follow him towards the correct parking stand.

Chapter 28

Tricia and Claire hug each other and tears of joy roll down Tricia's face. 'What's Mom crying for, we've landed?' Craig says, totally oblivious of the facts, which have made the landing possible.

Stuart brings the plane in slowly, as the batman waves his batons directing Stuart towards him, until he crosses his batons and Stuart stops the plane on its marks.

'Hawk two seven five,' Kate calls. 'Hawk two seven five,' Stuart replies.

'To kill the Engines move the two Engine Cut Off Switches below the Throttle Levers forward, and the Engines will stop.' 'Yes will do, and thanks once again.' Stuart moves the switches, and he hears the engines slowly whine down, and then silence.

He sits in his seat absolutely shattered, and quietly thinks to himself thank God that's over, and thank God we made it.

He sees four sets of stairs being moved towards the aircraft, two on the port side, and two on the starboard side.

The cabin crews unlock all four doors, and swing them back onto the side of the aircraft, as the stairs are moved towards the plane.

The luggage buggies are seen approaching the aircraft, and the bendy buses follow them. Normal activities seem to be underway in order to disembark the passengers as quickly as possible, as if the landing of the plane had just been routine, an everyday occurrence, and their jobs were to get the plane ready for its return flight.

The passengers gather their belongings together, and make for the doors on the port side of the aircraft. They thank the stewardesses for their help, and yet it was said more of a matter of fact than of a merciful thanks for everything, including saving their lives, but they can't wait to get out of here, and on with their holiday. Yet, they can also be forgiven for their attitude, for they were not fully aware of the situation they had been in. They knew something wasn't right, but they didn't know the full extent of their situation, and it was possibly as well they didn't.

The paramedics enter the plane, two to the front, and two to the back.
Zoe is with John at the front, and informs the paramedics he has slipped a disc in his back. One of the paramedics goes back to his ambulance, and returns with a flat board to slide under John, so they can lift him onto the stretcher. They wrap

him in a blanket, and lift him up, and slowly leave the plane down the staircase. 'I'll see you in the Hospital later,' Zoe shouts to John, as he leaves the plane. He waves his hand gently as they descend the stairs.

Dr Love supervises the paramedics as they place a heart monitor onto Martins chest, she has informed the paramedics at the rear of the plane of his condition. Eventually they lift him onto a stretcher, and remove him from the plane, and transfer him to hospital. 'Thank you so much for all your help,' Emma says to Doctor Love. 'That's all right, I was glad to be of assistance. I think he will recover, but he will need to take it easy for a while,' she replied, as she made her way back to her seat to get her two girls, and their hand luggage.

Stuart removes his headset, and climbs out of his seat. Tricia, Claire and Craig are among the last passengers still on the plane. Tricia makes her way to the front, just as Stuart opens the cockpit door. She runs the last few steps, and flings her arms around him, and squeezes him tight, and gives him a real passionate kiss.

'Wow,' Stuart says, in a state of unexpected shock, as he slowly lowers Tricia to the ground. Claire gives her dad a big hug, and finally the penny drops with Craig, as he realises it was his dad, who was flying the plane.

'Were you flying the Plane Dad?' Craig asks, as they all laugh at the fact he has just realised he was. 'Yes Son, how did I do?' 'Not too bad,' he replied as his dad picks him up. 'Marks out of ten.' 'Seven,' he says. 'As much as that, well gee thanks Son,' Stuart replies.

The stewardesses gather round Stuart, and say goodbye as they leave the plane. 'Thanks,' Zoe says, and gives Stuart a big kiss.

'Enjoy your Holiday, and see you on the return trip.' 'The first thing I want is a large cold Lager, and I think I might catch the bus back home. No offence,' he says, as he steps onto the staircase, and breathes in the lovely warm air, as the sunshine hits his face.

He can hear clapping, and people cheering from the bus, as he walks down the staircase holding Craig in his arms.

They all step onto the bus and are greeted with 'Well done mate,' 'Thanks,' and he gets slaps on his back from the passengers.

The smart businessman, who had been sitting behind Stuart on the plane said, 'I didn't know the Airline had spare passenger Pilots on their planes?' 'They don't,' Stuart replied. 'Well you must be able to fly other types of Aircraft?' 'No, I have never flown a Plane before.' 'You are kidding me, please say you are kidding?' 'No.'

The man went a deathly shade of white as Stuart smiles and says, 'Are you all right, you have gone a funny colour. Was it something I said? Give this man some air. I think he's going to faint.' The man was holding onto the pole by the door and slowly he slid down to the floor.

Oh, not again, Stuart thought as the bus pulled up at the terminal building. The driver opened the door and the fresh air came in, and revived the businessman. He slowly got to his feet as the other passengers stepped over him in their rush to get to the baggage hall first.

Stuart helps the man to his feet. 'Come on and sit here for a minute. I am sorry if I shocked you,' Stuart said.

The man just held his head between his knees for a few minutes, and then slowly sat up. 'How do you feel now?' Stuart asked. 'Ok I am getting there.'

A few seconds passed and he got to his feet. 'Are you ok now?' Stuart asked. 'Yes I'll be fine. Come on let's go.'

They all leave the bus, but Stuart was still a little concerned as they entered the terminal building and made their way to the baggage hall to wait for their luggage.

The usual melee ensues as the luggage comes through onto the endless conveyor belt. Everyone watching the suitcases, thinking I hope mine is next. Could this be the one, it looks like mine, may be not. Stuart doesn't have this problem for their suitcases are bright yellow, and Claire's is pink, and Craig's has a blue band round it. So he won't have any problems with spotting theirs, unless of course there is someone else with the identical cases, and one might suppose that is a chance in a million.

Dan Casper and his film crew have left the outside area of the airport, and made their way inside, in the hope of getting an interview with the hero of the day. They set up their camera close to the arrivals door, as the passengers slowly come through, all pushing their trolleys, piled high in some cases, giving the impression they were staying for ever, and not just two weeks. Some people seem to pack everything including the kitchen sink when they go on holiday, Dan thinks to himself as he waits.

The hall is filling up with people looking for their tour operator, and then slowly making their way outside to the waiting buses, but Dan still hasn't seen his hero.

Stuart finally spots his suitcases coming through onto the conveyor belt, and he grabs them as they come round, and places them onto his trolley, just as a man approaches him. 'I am Sam Shutt the Airport Manager,' the man says, as he introduces himself to Stuart, and they both shake hands.

'I think you are the guy who landed that plane a few minutes ago.' 'Yes,' Stuart says in reply. 'Well, may I thank you on behalf of everyone for the splendid job you did to day.' 'Thank you,' Stuart says.

'My Dad's a Hero,' Craig says. 'Yes he is Young Man, and if there is anything we can do for you, then you must say.' 'Well the only thing I want now is to get out of here, and checked into my Hotel, and have a cold Beer,' Stuart says. 'Right, well we hope you have a good one, and when you come back ask for me, and I shall see that you get VIP treatment for you and your family.' 'Right you're on, and thanks,' Stuart says, as they all make their way out into the arrivals hall.

Dan Caper spots Stuart, and approaches him, and stops him in his tracks, and puts the microphone to his face.

'I am Dan Casper of INN News. You are the Guy who has just landed the Plane from Birmingham England. Could I interview you?' Dan asks. 'Yes.' 'Ok we are going live now to Faro Airport,' the producer says to the television audience as Dan gets his que. 'Now,' the producer says in Dan's earpiece.

'I have with me the Pilot of the Plane which has just landed from Birmingham England, and who saved the lives of one hundred and fifty fellow passengers. You had us quite worried for a while, and we didn't think you were going to make it. What was going through your mind up there?' Dan asked.

'Exactly that, was I going to make it, it was very scary.' 'Have you ever flown that type of Aircraft before?' 'I have never flown an Aircraft.' 'That seems unbelievable.' 'Well, I can assure you it's true, but I wouldn't have made it if it wasn't for all the help I had from Kate in the Control Tower. She was brilliant, and I just followed her instructions.' 'How come you were designated to take over?' 'I wasn't. The Co Pilot John Cutler, as a small reward for helping him out on his way to the Airport, had invited me into the Cockpit, when both Pilots were taken ill, so someone had to do something or we would all have died.' 'Well, you did a splendid job.' 'Well thanks, but it was just a Million to One Chance of ever happening, and I hope it never happens to me again.' 'What are your plans now. Are you thinking of becoming a Pilot?' 'No way. I think I shall stick to Teaching.' 'Well enjoy your Holiday.'

Stuart pushes his trolley off and out into the sunshine, followed by Tricia and the family, all happy and looking forward to their holiday and to getting his cold beer.

Meanwhile, Martin and John have had their treatment in the hospital in Faro, and find themselves together in a twin bedded room. 'You made an excellent job of landing the Plane under the circumstances,' John says to Martin. 'I didn't land the Plane,' Martin replies. 'If you didn't, and I didn't, then, ...oh my God, who did.......................'

I would like to thank my wife Liz for all her support in writing this book. For all her help with the editorial work and the encouragement to continue with it over these last two years.

ISBN 141209619-7